SCATTERED
Tales

R. HENRY PRICE

Also by R. Henry Price

Problem Book in Relativity and Gravitation (1975)
A. P. Lightman, W. H. Press, R. H. Price and S. A. Teukolsky,
Princeton University Press

Black Holes: The Membrane Paradigm (1986)
K.S. Thorne, R. H. Price and D. A. Macdonald,
Yale University Press

The Future of Spacetime (2002)
S. Hawking, K. S. Thorne, I. Novikov,
T. Ferris, Alan Lightman, Richard Price
W. W. Norton

Mentis and Ethos (2023)
R. Henry Price
Dorrance Publishing Co
Pittsburgh, PA

The Allure of an Ending (2025)
R. Henry Price
Glass Spider Publishing
Ogden, UT

*To my collaborators and critics, Lin and Lorna.
And to Gavi who, at age nine, was my first collaborator.*

TABLE OF CONTENTS

PREFACE

I hate prefaces. For one thing, I've never really understood the differences: preface, introduction, or foreword. (I think a prologue is just a warm-up and doesn't belong in this list.) The root of my dislike of front matter is my pathologically overdeveloped fear of cutting any corner, of skipping any step. If I didn't read everything starting with the ISBN, I know that people would furtively point to me on the street and whisper behind their hands that I was the guy who skipped the preface, introduction, or foreword.

So I read them and resented them as barriers that needed to be surmounted to get to the "good stuff" or the discovery that the stuff isn't so good. Reader, you can be certain, therefore, that this preface is the lowest of barriers. It is simply an attempt to explain what this book is not.

For it is not a collection of short stories. The pieces packaged here are not all stories, and they are not all short, and I think that "collection" may be less appropriate than a word like "assemblage" (although "trove" is appealing).

I shied away from "collection" because I read somewhere (a preface?) that items in a collection should be related by a common theme. The only commonality in the following pages is that all items are thought to be interesting by the author and those of his friends and colleagues who were too slow in changing their email addresses. There is no real commonality; there is variety. I like to think that the pieces here are varied enough that any reader can find something to like and something to complain about.

Having clarified, or at least stated, what this gathering of writings is not, I will self-indulgently stab at clarifying, or at least commenting on, some background for the contributions that may be useful. It may not be, so dear Reader, please feel free to skip to the good stuff or the disappointment. No one will know.

Of the thirteen items to follow, ten are "just" fiction. Many are (or were intended to be) humorous, even silly ("Buster"), in some others the humor is a garnish, not the main ingredient and in a few any humor was unintentional.

One of the stories ("Through Africa…") is a hand-on-heart-true autobiographical travelogue. Though the style is meant to be humorous, the facts themselves need little help in that direction. Its reason for being is presented in a brief remark at the beginning of the piece, so no more need be said here.

Two of the pieces are quasi-scientific. "Slime Mold" is an attempt to wring a few laughs from the astonishing cellular slime mold *Dictyostelium discoideum*. This organism has fascinated me since I learned of it a long time ago (more specificity of "long" is lost to memory). Originally, the fascination came from wondering how the amoebae decided who would be the leader when they aggregated into a single multicellular organism. That sort of inter-amoeba communication is the device in Part II of the brace of "Slime Mold" writings.

Part I is the more interesting of the two writings. The intended humor is not meant to obscure the miraculous nature of these creatures and comes mostly from the affectionate mocking of scientific writing style. The mocking would not excuse scientific misrepresentations, so I spent quite a few days reading summary articles and primary papers on *D. discoideum*. Truth be told, I had trouble pulling myself away from the topic. The leadership of the multicellular aggregate is only the beginning!

The second somewhat scientific short contribution—"Was the Universe Always There?"—is very different in style and content. I'd like to think it shows that our understanding of the physical world has come to a point at which it may be hard to distinguish science from faith. Although this is not a point hammered on in the contribution, our "understanding" that there is a beginning of time, that the Universe is infinite, and such, is the result of having faith in mathematics and accepting what would seem to be as unacceptable as the miracles of *D. discoideum*.

The remainder of this prefatial low barrier is brief comments on the ten fictional items.

"Buster" (the silly story) is just me allowing myself the feeling of superiority and sympathy for an unreliable narrator. Here the narrator is not so much off the mark as he is putting far too much trust in his aim.

"Robby" is near-future science fiction. I am not big on science fiction, although snarky remarks to that effect have been made about the physics papers from my previous career. In "Robby," I am trying to use the science fiction as a background to a human story. (This is also very much the case in my novel *The Allure of an Ending*.)

The inspirations for most of the stories are scattered.

"Multiple Tracks" had its seed in the behavior of a glib friend who boasted of the fables he would spin to airplane seatmate strangers who made the mistake of boring him with their opinions.

The seed of "The Meadow" was a story my son-in-law told me about a friend who failed to thrive as an adult and lived in his mother's Manhattan apartment, wasting his life reviewing video games. I gave him a backstory. He is recognizable as Bear in the story, but just barely. As any author knows, characters, once introduced take over; the author is only there as a reporter.

"The Carton" grew from two very different seeds. A discussion with friends on the meaning of "home" was stuck in my mind when my curiosity about the structure and history of cardboard led me to the Wikipedia article and the working of "flutes" in cardboard. Thus entered Randy and his cardboard home. Randy took over, told his story, and reminded me that people could be as surprising as *D. discoideum* or cosmological models. The story is fiction, but I think that what it says about human relations rings very true.

"Half Wittgenstein" is an exercise in ridiculing both the stereotypical self-absorption at the top of the academic tower, and the disconnected mindlessness of young tech dwellers. This story strengthens my belief that writing can spill over into psychoanalysis. I suspect this tale fed on dormant resentment of Wittgenstein from my first year at college.

At the start of "Strutting and Fretting," there is an *"Author's explicatio."* Although the work overall is (meta)fiction, that introductory justification is fictional only in its humorous self-important style. It explains what I was trying to do, a bit more than to supply laughs. No more about it need be said here.

Perhaps there are subconscious autobiographical elements in everything an author writes, but those elements are not sub in "The Red Digits." I see those red numbers and the mountain range of quilts every morning. Less frequently I see the deeper meaning of the story, the triviality of the everyday fleeting issues that seem so important and their contrast with what really matters.

I like to think that I can write in very different styles. Surely some of the pieces below confirm that, since I did not claim "write well." "Nita" is my attempt at writing a Scandi noir story. It was an education, requiring five drafts to wash away the bad jokes and word play. I think I finally tossed away all that bathwater without losing a gloomy baby haunted by the meaning of justice.

Do I really have to explain the motivation for "Agency," at least for the framing story?

Most of the items in this assemblage were written after I had started to take nonscientific writing seriously in 2022. Two of the stories date from much earlier, in particular "The Meadow," which was written in 2004 and changed very little when it was freshened in 2025. Buster also dates back twenty years or so, but has been significantly improved, or anyway changed, when rewritten in 2025. The African travelogue was written in the late summer of 2001, immediately after the events it describes, before the imperfection of memory introduced noise.

You've made it over the low barrier, so you deserve to have what follows entertain you. I hope it does; I hope you have as much enjoyment reading it as I did writing it.

THE CARTON

"What the hell?!"

"Hey, Arlene. Not doing any damage. Just looking. Your cardboard is different from mine."

"So you destroying mine?"

"Just peeling back a small patch to look at the flute."

"You a really strange one Randy. You goddamn lucky I watch out for you. What the hell's a flute?"

"It's this pleated paper, the corrugations, that keep the flat sheets of the cardboard apart. It's what makes our boxes so strong. Pretty damn interesting, eh? Pretty damn clever."

"Don't take much to muse you Randy. But I'll be first to admit—hell, only one—you a clever son of a bitch—what you done with that packing box."

When Randy realized that he'd be living on the street for a while, he figured why not make the best of it? Get the biggest possible carton for starters. So he slipped some pills to one of the delivery drivers for the French-ish restaurant, *Le Cygne Chanteur*, five blocks down on the other side of the street. Very different from Randy's neighborhood. The driver would let him know when something was delivered in an especially large cardboard carton.

Maybe four weeks later the driver said he had good news—for another three pills. A big commercial refrigeration unit had been delivered. It was the end of his deliveries, the end of the workday.

The driver sat down on the entrance step of one of the abandoned storefronts. Took two cigarettes out of a pack, lit both, gave one to Randy. The driver watched the smoke and became pensive, mellow, in a mood to talk about fourteen years of delivering restaurant equipment. The temperature starting to drop and the light starting to fade encouraged reflections.

"Y'know, big stuff, like that Samsung 49 cube battleship, usedta ship without carboard, just thick plastic wrapping. Thing is they can get banged up. A nightmare. Restaurant won't take delivery. We're stuck taking it back and bitching about who's gotta pay. So some dude at Samsung who probably knows next to nothing. Real close next to. Asks how come we don't have this kind of shit hitting the fan with regular fridges and stuff. Some working stiff, too smart for management, tells him corrugated cardboard is the original bang-up protector. The guy in the tie counts beans. Wow, cardboards's gonna cost. But then remembers what it's been costing for returns. So bada and bing, they ship them in huge cardboard containers."

Randy exhaled thoughtfully and said, "Lucky me."

"You hit the nail Randy. Cmon. You can't drag that monster box a half mile. Walk with me to the *Stinking Swan* and I'll take you and the box back in the truck."

"That what the name of the restaurant means? The *Stinking Swan*?"

"Had a Canadian tell us it's the *Singing Swan*. Guys I work with like our translation better. More accurate, you ask me."

That was four years ago. Randy used the box as his castle. Four and a half feet high, so he couldn't stand in it but standing was for outside anyway. His floor was sidewalk, and he had a lot of it; the box was more than six and a half feet wide. When he was first setting it up he thought about orienting it vertically, but why? And it would attract too much attention sticking up like a cardboard skyscraper.

Randy took the thick plastic wrapping and used it with duct tape to waterproof his container. Corrugated was great until it got wet, now it wouldn't. He then scavenged some corrugated slabs here and there and duct-taped them to all sides, making the container strong enough to ward off the occasional kick or the frequent strong wind.

Randy's new truck driver friend had dropped off a couple of slabs of polyurethane foam that had been used for protection during shipping. Two of them became protection from the sidewalk roughness and cold under his sleeping bag. It was a bed no worse than what Randy remembered of his banker days.

In the summer he left the front cardboard flap open, but mostly stayed outside for whatever breeze there was. He would drag the lawn chair from his carton to the shade and cool of the nearby overpass. It was a gathering place of those from the street's boxes, neighborly but silent. The winter was different. He took joy in hearing the wind, in being inside, protected and warm.

Arleen had watched him build his corrugated home. She wasn't interested in copying, and probably couldn't, but she had been on the street a long time and had never seen anything like it.

"Arlene, this will be St. Samsung by the overpass, the pride of Center Street Estates."

She didn't understand the joke. It didn't matter. There were different types on the street, and here was a new one. He wasn't a threat or a soft touch, but she liked him and told him in her cigarette raspy voice that she would watch out for his home when he was away. She would keep away those who would steal from their corner of the Estates. Arlene was big, fast and known to have knives and skills. More important she was crazy enough to use knives and skills. The crazy might have been real or her street-useful act. Reputation was more important than reality. Randy had seen that also in the corporate world.

It was important to have friends on the street. When he had cigarettes Randy gave one to Arlene to smoke between coughs. Better than her usual source. Her nose bore burn evidence of the street butts she would light. They almost never spoke. Communication was physical presence. Sometimes gestures.

Arlene was his security guard when he left St. Samsung for a meal or shower in the shelter two blocks away. Nothing was ever missing from his small stash when he returned. His chalk mark calendar said he'd been on the street for almost four years. Arlene's cough was worse now, much worse, and sometimes brought up blood. He wasn't counting on her being around much longer. Nor was Arlene. Randy understood that the street people took comfort in not having to plan for the future.

Their plans were for the day, and the day could surprise them, the night more so.

A night of strong winds collapsed Arlene's carton. Randy heard its wind driven flapping and investigated. Arlene had pulled her sleeping bag from her collapsing home and was huddled in it on the street. Randy tried to speak to her but the wind was too strong. He made a come-with-me gesture. She tried to take her sleeping bag, but she was shivering too violently to control her hands. Randy pushed her inside his wind defying carton and followed with her sleeping bag. He took one of his foam slabs and laid it out for her sleeping bag. After ten minutes, the shivering stopped. He listened for breathing, before trying for sleep again.

In the morning Randy told her that she could stay that night. The weather was supposed to break, and Arlene would be able to repair her carton the following day. But they both felt awkward sharing a space, and Arlene managed to make it through the next night inside the collapsed carton of her home.

She never came right out and thanked Randy. Saying thanks was reserved for donors to a hat left on the sidewalk and seeded with a few quarters and a dollar bill. To the street people thanks had the stink of insincerity. Their communication needs were simple, and rarely required words. Randy understood.

Randy learned that all of them said they were different, and he stopped saying he was. But he couldn't help thinking it when the past tapped him on the shoulder that second year. A private detective had located him—not that hard really, he never used a fake name. The PI gave him an envelope. He wouldn't answer questions, just pointed at the envelope, "It's in there. Read it."

Randy's father had died. Too late to attend the funeral. There was the matter of the will. The letter was from Rodney Whitner, his father's lawyer for more than fifteen years. He and Randy knew each other, at least what they looked like. He knew that Randy would not want to travel hundreds of miles if it could be done by a gofer or mail to the homeless shelter. It couldn't. The lawyer explained that there was an "issue" that would come up based on the will. Negotiations would go on for a few days and new papers would have to be signed. Too much back and forth for it to be done remotely.

The letter included instructions for Randy to claim an open ticket on United waiting at the airport along with cash enough for minor expenses during travel and a taxi to the airport. He was to call the lawyer to let him know when he'd be landing. A car would meet him.

There really wasn't a choice except to get it over with. He didn't mind the 300 miles as much as the four years. Back to before the banking world, back before the pills to numb the pain of that world. He looked around at the cardboard tenements of Center Street Estates. No one said that life was easy.

Randy walked to the shelter and asked to use the phone in the office. Long distance, but he would call collect. Natalie worried about her flock, but Randy was a smaller worry than most. She trusted him and left the office to give him privacy he didn't need.

He had not been on the street so long that he had forgotten how the modern world worked. He first called the airline, checked that there was a ticket being held for him and asked for the time of the next few flights. He chose one that would give him plenty of time to make it to the airport. No point in cutting it close. No pressure from his busy schedule. Then there was the memory of packing for a trip. Yet another advantage of life on the street.

He thanked Natalie, asked to take a shower and gave her five dollars as a contribution to the towel fund. Natalie looked at his roll of bills and at him.

"Relax. Didn't rob a bank, Natalie. My father died. Gotta be there for the will stuff. They sent money for travel."

"Sorry to hear about your loss, Randy."

"Yeah, thanks."

Mostly dry he walked through the cold a few blocks toward the *Swan* to catch a cab. They didn't stop near the Estates.

Three hours later a crisply uniformed chauffeur was holding a sign *Randolph Westbrook* neatly stenciled. Randy, rumpled and threadbare, approached and went off with him. In an age of non-conformist tech billionaires the stares were brief.

The chauffeur was trying to decide whether Randy was a regular guy and might want to talk on the long ride. But he played it safe, the right move since O'Hare made Randy retract into the past. With his attention elsewhere he automatically got into the rear seat of the Lincoln limousine and watched the once familiar past as he sunk back over his head into the depths. No thought to the contrast of the leather and silence with where he had started the trip.

The car dropped him off in the portico. No one answered the door when he rang. He waited but not long enough; it was a big house. On either side of the front door were large snake plants chosen by the Japanese gardener/feng shui adviser, whose English was a mystery. When Randy lived in this house there was always a house key buried inconspicuously in the left planter. He started to dig, when the door was opened by a fiftyish housekeeper wearing a black uniform and scowl. She figured out who it must be pawing at the dirt in the planter.

"Randolph?"

"Right. I'm Randy. You're new."

"I've been working here for two years."

Randy thought "Right, she's new," but kept quiet. She led him to the living room, though the layout was indelible in his mind and too frequently in his dreams. He sat and looked around at what little had changed. Something that had changed for the much worse was his mother who was descending the staircase holding a scotch.

"Evening, Mom. You look fabulous."

"Bullshit as usual, Randy. I know that I scare children. Age has caught up. It's toying with me like a housecat. Not like the cardiac tiger that mercifully ripped up your father… what was it? Three weeks ago?"

She took a long sip, emptying the glass, and walked toward the sideboard where a bottle of Johnny Walker Blue was already at half-mast.

"Drink, Randy?"

"Thanks, Mom, but no. Don't take chances with anything addictive."

"Even ciggies?" she said taking one for herself from a silver box.

"Gimme one please. Cigarettes are not addictive. Just look at the testimony of RJ Reynolds."

She sat, gracefully as always, in the sofa facing him. In the better light she looked worse.

"You know that your father left you nothing. Did Rodney tell you that?"

"Didn't mention it. Didn't have to. Dad said he'd leave me nothing and I would rot in hell. He was a man of his word. Couldn't arrange for the hell part. Some might disagree."

"Your father was a difficult man."

"Yeah, Hitler and Stalin too. Enough. Where's the princess?"

"Your sister will not be joining us for dinner, but Rodney will. He wants to talk to you. For Christ's sake Randy open your mind. He's on your side."

"Great. Plenty of room over here."

They sat, smoking in silence. Not comfortable, not uncomfortable. Both were used to long stretches without conversation, though for different reasons.

The humorless housekeeper answered the door when Rodney Whitmer arrived not long after 6:30.

"Evelynne, always nice to see you."

"Evening Rodney. Thank you for not telling me how well I look. An honest lawyer! Age of miracles."

"Randy, it's been a while. Thank you for coming."

Randy said nothing but nodded in acknowledgment. No point in being rude. And Randy had never disliked the lawyer, had always suspected that he was a check on his father's worst impulses. Anyway, Randy had it on good authority that the lawyer was on his side.

There wasn't much talk at dinner. Randy was smart enough to know that his body was out of practice with rich food, and exercised, perhaps flaunted, self-discipline. His mother was getting her calories from Johnny Walker. The lawyer was enjoying the food but felt awkward, so business talk started with the coffee and tiramisu.

"Randy, aside from a few small items, charities, long time staff, your father left everything to your mother. Let me save you the task of asking the obvious: why are you here?"

"All ears."

"Randy, in the vernacular of the young - full confession: I am now your mother's lawyer; we have signed a contract. As before—when I was your father's attorney—my job is legal advice. I don't make what you might call strategy decisions. Only—sometimes—suggestions. Inviting you here was your mother's idea. She insisted on it."

"Still all ears. Now they're even listening."

"It's not about your father's last testament; it's about the future. Your mother feels that she doesn't have much time ..."

Evelynne interrupted.

"Thank God. Can't wait."

The lawyer continued.

"Your father bequeathed the bulk of his estate to her. We can talk about the size of that bulk, but it's probably not crucial as long as you understand—and I'm sure you do—that the estate is enormous. You know he started out with a big inheritance, built up several businesses, made shrewd investments,..."

"Yeah, Rodney. Got it. Huge. Knew that. Please get on with it."

"The future is where I'm getting on to. Very soon—and she's hoping that it's tomorrow—she has to make up her own will. She has the difficult task of deciding where this money should go."

Randy thought "poor Mom," but kept quiet. This was too important, and he felt the birth of foreboding. The lawyer continued.

"The list of possible beneficiaries includes a few alienated distant relatives—your family seems to have trouble getting along—a few favorite charities, your sister Ava, and you."

"Rodney. Stop. Let me shorten your list. I don't want it. I would donate it to charity. So save me the paperwork and just have that written in; my part goes to some charity. You decide. If you know any charity my father hated choose that one. Where do I sign?"

The lawyer looked uncomfortably around, especially at Evelynne who could hold her scotch well enough to take the hint. She rose from the table and said, "Lady MacBeth exits stage left."

She was slightly shaky as she tackled the staircase ascent. Randy watched, worried. She was his mother. It was the lawyer's turn again.

"Randy, here's the complication. Your mother and Ava don't get along very well."

"Glory be. I had no idea."

It was a slipup. Randy had meant to be serious, now felt foolish.

Randy had lived through the background. Way too young Ava had fallen for Bruce, movie star looks, nice guy, community college. Evelynne said he wasn't going anywhere and Ava had to find someone with a future. Ava shrugged at the loss of a big wedding and eloped. King Harold, father and husband, said no problem. He would give Bruce a future and mold him to fit it. The molding drove Bruce away. He just wasn't the sort of clay Harold could work with.

Evelynne had been harsher in her judgments of Bruce. Insisting she knew what was best for her only daughter. Ava had to blame someone for the disaster. Her mother raised her hand and cried out "Me, me!" Ava, a divorcée at 23, had trouble getting traction in her life, and decided to blame her mother for pretty much everything. The alternative, seeing that it was her own fault, didn't appeal.

King Harold was having his own problems and didn't take sides. The molding of Randy had gone even worse than with Bruce.

Randy apologized for his wiseass remark. The lawyer shrugged it off and continued.

"Evelynne is considering not bequeathing anything to Ava."

Up to this point Randy had been observing from a distance. Now he tensed up for whatever was to come. It wouldn't be good, and whatever it was triggered his I don't need this shit switch. It wasn't a time for a stupid remark. The lawyer had paused to let it all hit Randy. He continued.

"All to me? Then why not all to charity?"

"Ava is why not. She is worried, and she's not going to sit back and just let that money go to charity. Or to you."

"Rodney, excuse the stupid comment, but it's not her decision, right?"

"Ava's scheming to make it her decision. How? Fortunately, she revealed her plan in a screaming fit to frighten her mother. The plan—not that hard to guess—is that during probate her legal team will argue that leaving almost a billion dollars to a homeless son is *prima facie* evidence that your mother was not *compos mentis*. *Prima facie* means—"

"Yeah, yeah. I know what it means. Also *compos mentis*."

"The court could nullify the will and there's no telling what it might decide for the money. My best guess is that Ava will go for conservatorship. She'll ask the court to declare her your guardian. Her legal team will present evidence of your drug use and your life on the street. Their people will bribe a few on the street to testify that you had done dangerous things. They will make the case that you would use the money to do God knows what.

"Acting on behalf of your deceased mother's written wishes I would fight those efforts."

"Rodney, what are the chances?"

"You have any dice?"

"No. Don't have a gun either, thank God. What can we do?"

"I'm going to make a strange suggestion: We immediately have a court declare me your guardian. If we pull it off, Ava's argument vanishes that you would be irresponsible, maybe dangerous, with the money."

Sitting in a room from the past Randy had felt free of the past. He wondered whether anyone ever was.

It was the age of scams. Could he trust Rodney? He didn't know. Why did he care since he didn't care about the money. Long unused circuits in his brain were connecting. The smarts that had made him such a success before he became such a failure. The smarts alerted him that as his guardian Rodney could pull him off the street and have him put into some institution.

Rodney saw that Randy was thinking and waited. This was no time for rushing. Also not for delicacy.

"Rodney, how do I know you won't use the conservatorship to put me away in some adult daycare center and relieve yourself of the burden of actually watching out for me?"

"Good question, and I'm glad you're clever Randy again. We can protect you from my dark schemes by creating a document limiting what I can do about your personal freedom, and conditions that would be involved."

Nothing was for sure, but two bad choices very likely. In a year, maybe less, he would have either Rodney or Ava as a guardian.

"Rodney, could we wait till after my mother's funeral to see what Ava's going to do?"

"We could but we'd be taking a chance of a legal battle over conservatorship. Ava's team against mine. If we're going to do it, we should do it now."

"Rodney, can you give me two thousand against a promissory note pending the settlement of my mother's estate."

"Happy to."

Randy would pay an independent attorney to draw up the document limiting Rodney.

"Okay. Rodney. Let's get it over with. I choose you. Congratulations and sympathy.

Will I have to return here?"

"Yes, almost certainly."

"Okay, if it has to be. Now could you please get me the hell out of here."

Rodney telephoned an always on call assistant, arranged for the first flight out of O'Hare and for a car. The flight got him back to O'Hare at 2 a.m. He caught a cab, but in a repetition of the morning experience the cabbie wouldn't enter his neighborhood. He was dropped off four blocks away. An eight-minute walk.

The night was cold and windy. He was wearing his wool overcoat from long ago. It was made for looks not for protection. He pulled up the collar, hunched his shoulders and stuffed his hands deep into the pockets. He could tolerate eight minutes of this.

He saw the overpass, the cartons. He saw his Samsung home, longed to be inside, and cried.

ROBBY

Other vehicles were ghosts sharing the evening. The transport drove forward between the two blurred cones of its headlights.

"How much longer until we get there?"

"Relax Robby. They're going to fix you up just fine. There's no rush; they told me it's not going to get any worse for days. Maybe weeks."

"You believed them?"

"More or less. What they say makes some sense. Besides, why would they lie?"

Daniels looked out the window. The gray evening mist outside fit the feeling inside the transport. They would lie, just as he was doing.

Robby was strapped in a supine position to a large flat palette, itself fastened to the floor of the transport. From his position Robby could see only the ceiling. Daniels was seated on a bench attached to the side of the vehicle. He was a rule follower, but he unfastened the seat belt so that he could slide over to be closer to Robby, and could slide away to look out the side window.

"Can you tell where we are?"

"Not sure by looking out the window. Why are you so curious?"

"Curiosity is what we're all about. Input."

"Robby, it doesn't seem like important input, where we are."

"To you, no. To me, very important. I want to know how long until we arrive, because I want to know how long I've got. I know it's the end."

Daniels looked away, concentrating on what he could see of the road through the misted window. After a few moments, he turned away from the window and

clicked the mid-telephoto option on his glasses so that he could read the dashboard display.

"We'll be there in about twenty minutes."

"Thank you for letting me know. When you called HMRA, what were their actual words?"

"I'd rather not say, Robby, since nothing is certain. I wouldn't want to worry you unnecessarily, or—maybe worse—give you false hope. It is what it is, and we'll soon know."

"I was trained to hear between lines, and I've just heard that it's over for me."

"Now Robby…"

"No tears. I don't do tears. We knew this would be coming when I first arrived seven years ago."

"Seven years? No way, Robby. Seven years?"

"You know that I never make an error with factual data. Yes. Seven years. I remember getting to know you during the first year. Training sometimes takes two years, but after one year the training was complete."

"You mean I'm so simple that I wasn't a challenge."

"No. Not simple. Consistent. You are very consistent. After a year I could predict very well what you wanted and what was going on in your mind."

"What do you predict now?"

"I predict that you're going to miss me at first, but you'll find a replacement for me soon enough."

"No, Robby. You cannot be replaced. I don't think I'll ever be able to replace your singing around the house. I would call out the name of a song and you could sing it beautifully."

"Dr. Daniels, perhaps you noticed that I never asked you to sing after the first time."

"Another thing I'll miss, Robby, is your sense of humor."

"I don't have a sense of humor. You observed an optional-behavior program."

Daniels had nothing to say. He looked away again.

"How long before you replace me?"

"I'll think about that if and when I need to."

"I cannot picture you with another robot."

"Is this jealousy? Robby, you're not capable of jealousy."

"No, I am not. But I am designed to be curious, always wanting new input. I stated that I cannot picture you with another robot. It was a statement about the limitations of my visualization. My replacement might have upgraded visualization, possibly with the ability you call imagination."

After a long pause Robby added, "When you told me you were going to marry Barbara I could not picture that either. I could not picture what it would be like having her come into the home."

"That was, what, almost four years ago?"

"Yes, almost four years. I learned a lot about Barbara during her first year in our home. Of course, I was already trained on you. When she moved in I needed to train on her. Understanding her actions was part of my obligation-set for you. She was more difficult than you. She was very inconsistent."

"Yes. I noticed you seemed good at understanding what she wanted, but still you did not treat her the way you treated me. I suppose that's all in your chips."

"Well, firmware, but basically, yes. And it was not my job to make suggestions and help her with decisions; those actions were strictly for you. It was my job to do what she wanted unless it was not what you would have wanted. That difference may be interpreted by a Sapien as being unfriendly, like not smiling."

"Yeah, maybe Barbara was expecting a smile. She complained about your attitude."

"Dr. Daniels, you know that I am incapable of having attitudes. She was just misinterpreting my behavior."

"Perhaps you are misinterpreting *her* behavior."

"How can I misinterpret that she complained about me, and she never smiled when I was around?"

They both fell quiet. Daniels was thinking. Robby was processing.

"Dr. Daniels. You are going to die. How do you feel about it?"

"Feel about it? I don't know how I feel about it. How do you feel about the possibility of being powered down?"

"How do I feel? I don't know how I feel because I don't know what a feeling is. You were certainly aware of that."

"Sorry, I keep forgetting that …"

"Is it good to have feelings?"

"Without feelings I wouldn't be a Sapien. I would miss the joys of life, so I guess it's good to have feelings."

"I know that there are bad feelings also. Despite this, if you could choose you would choose to have feelings?"

"A choice? I've never thought about having a choice. Yes, I'm pretty sure I would choose to have feelings."

"Can you control your feelings?"

"No. A bit. Not much."

"So, you would choose to have something you can't control."

Robby paused. Perhaps processing. He understood that a pause was appropriate behavior. Very soon after it would be appropriate to continue with a new question.

"Dr. Daniels, when you first met Barbara what were your feelings?"

Daniels kept quiet for almost a full minute. Robby waited with his unlimited patience. Daniels knew where Robby was going with the questions but decided: Fine. Let him go wherever.

"My feelings were very good, Robby. I was happy. Very happy."

"You were not happy before you met Barbara?"

"Well, yes. I guess I thought I was happy. It's hard to understand feelings. Lucky you, no feelings. Maybe I was lonely. More than I realized. I don't know."

"What does it mean to be lonely?"

"You have no one to share your thoughts and feelings."

"But you don't understand your feelings. How can you share them?"

"I don't know. Maybe you don't have to understand to share."

"And you shared your thoughts. Why did you want to share your thoughts?"

"I don't know. Maybe I wanted feedback. Maybe I wanted to try out an idea and get the opinion of a sharer."

"Barbara was not a scientist like you. Was she good at judging new ideas anyway?"

Daniels paused. He was now sure where this was going but wasn't about to be bullied by Robby.

"No. She wasn't good with new ideas. She wasn't flexible that way."

"Am I good at judging new ideas?"

"Yes, you have a great deal of knowledge stored and logical circuits to connect new ideas. I often did share ideas with you, and valued your feedback."

"But it was not enough?"

"I don't know. You're asking me why I do things, and I don't always understand why I do things."

"So you never understood why you thought you needed Barbara?"

"No damn it. I'm not like you. I make mistakes."

There were two officers of the HMRA in the front of the transport. A driver and a security/admin technician. The driver did not turn around when Daniels and Robby entered, even when the technician secured them. Daniels could see only the back of the driver's head above the seat. It seemed to be a large head, balding under the headphones. The technician was a mid-career officer whose age seemed appropriate for the rank. Her behavior was consistent with her appearance: stout body, short light brown hair, neutral expression. Not too aggressive, not too familiar. It was the face of someone good at dealing with events in the HMRA transport. Daniels appreciated the lack of chatter.

"Excuse me, Lieutenant, how much more time to the destination?"

Daniels knew the time but wanted an interruption in Robby's questioning.

"About twelve minutes, Dr. Daniels. As long as we're talking, let's go over the procedure you will follow when we arrive."

"I already know the procedure. I watched the videomail. Twice."

"Thank you for following directives. Unfortunately, I am required to go over the procedure with you anyway. Those are the rules."

Ordinarily, Daniels would have been annoyed, and possibly rude, at the waste of time. But the break from Robby's interrogation was welcome. Daniels signaled to the technician to go ahead. When she finished her memorized speech, she told Daniels "You'll need to fill out the HMRA transfer form."

"I did that and sent it in."

"Hold on," she said, as she checked. "Yes, you did. Good. Thank you." She updated the estimated time, now ten minutes, for their arrival.

Robby inferred that he could continue. He assumed that Daniels had forgotten just where they were in their interchange.

"We were discussing Barbara. Was there a change during the marriage?"

"A change in what?"

"Your feelings about her."

Daniels wished the questions would stop but wasn't going to stop answering them.

"Yes, my feelings about her changed."

"I believe that always happens when people spend a great deal of time together. Was it that you are no longer special to each other?"

"Maybe. I don't know."

"When she was no longer special to you? Did you get bored with her?"

"No! Not bored."

"What were your feelings, if not bored?"

"Just… I don't know. No longer excited."

"I noticed that you and Barbara began to have fights in the third year of marriage."

"No! Not fights. We had serious disagreements."

"Did you have disagreements during the first few months you knew her?"

"No. Nothing serious. I don't think so. I can't really remember."

"So, in the third year of marriage there must have been new

things to disagree about."

Daniels looked out the side window again. He could order Robby to stop speaking, but didn't. He was being sensitive to Robby's looming depowering. But why should he care?

Robby understood that Daniels turning away meant that he wanted Robby to stop asking him questions. When Daniels turned back, Robby took this as a signal to continue. He repeated his question.

"You had new things to disagree about later on?"

"I'm not sure. Perhaps."

"Was *I* an issue in the disagreements? Barbara mentioned me often in these serious disagreements."

"No. Okay. Sometimes. Yes, you sometimes were a subject of discussion."

"Did your affair with Vicky start because you were having serious disagreements with Barbara, or because Barbara no longer excited you?"

Daniels turned away again. His glasses were still in mid-telephoto mode so he stared at the dashboard display. Another six minutes.

Of course, Robby would know about the affair. He monitored Daniels' phone conversations and noticed little details that a Sapien would not notice. But Robby would notice. Robby had never mentioned it though of course he would know. Of course he would know, he would know about Vicky. But how did Barbara know? In the last month before they split, it was clear that Barbara knew.

Daniels had been very careful. Things had been bad enough with Barbara, and Daniels knew much of the fault was his. His affair with Vicky was not a grand romance; it was just a fling. Just an escape from the waning excitement. The fact that it was *just* an affair made it worse. It made Barbara's bitter accusations about his character valid. Daniels was a louse. He would admit it to himself, but could not tolerate hearing it over and over from Barbara.

But how had Barbara found out?

Robby was asking why the affair started.

"I don't know why it started. Yeah, maybe I was looking for new excitement."

"Why did it end?"

"I don't know why it ended. Once Barbara knew…"

"Did it hurt?"

"The end of the affair? No. It was a minor thing except for the effect on Barbara."

"Did the end of the marriage hurt?"

"The marriage? Yes. It hurt. Not like hitting my thumb with a hammer. It hurt in another way. It hurt the way I thought about myself. I guess, it made me feel that the new man she was seeing must be better than I am.

"It hurt mostly because I was so stupid to have that fling with Vicky. If Barbara had never learned of it I think everything would have settled down. I would choose a comfortable life without excitement. But she found out, so the choice wasn't mine."

Daniels felt the transport stop. The HMRA technical officer announced that they had just arrived. She then walked through the transport, opened the doors, and hopped down to the ground, offering Daniels a hand to steady his descent.

"Goodbye, Dr. Daniels," Robby cried out.

Daniels did not answer.

STRUTTING AND FRETTING

(A Metafictional Play in One Act, Three Scenes)

Author's explicatio: I was reading very much at random through the 10 percent free samples of books available from an internet vendor. There was no particular order to my rummaging, so there was no particular reason I stumbled across a particularly arcane work of Cormac McCarthy, *The Stonemason*, the earlier of his two published plays. Since the free sample was not many pages, each of them became important, and I read what I might otherwise not have in the first few of the stingily proffered pages: the cast of characters and the stage directions.

That front matter gave a running start to the story. We know, for example, from the description of character Mary Weaver as Big Ben's mistress, that Big Ben got around. From the stage directions and description of the setting, we may suspect that McCarthy, stepping away from the road he conquered with his prized novels, is unsure enough to ask for forbearance from his audience. He extends this request and perhaps displays his erudition (let us not throw stones) with *"As the mathematician Gauss said to his contemporaries: Go forward and faith will come to you."*

Though I lacked faith in the arrival of faith, I said to myself that it might be interesting, just as a challenge you understand, to go forward beyond an informative cast of characters and stage settings, to tell the whole story in these elements, the cast of characters and the stage setting. Similes with the DNA in a single human cell cry out to be cited but will not be heeded.

I was attracted by the possibility that this may never have been done before although, Gauss help me, lots of strange things have been done in the name of metafiction. There is *Pale Fire*, which seems to me a game Nabokov has played, caveat lector. Then there is the Barth story *Frame-Tale* printed on a Möbius strip for the obedient reader with scissors and tape.

Anyway, that's how it started out, a metafictional play. I invite you to judge how it ended up.

Going, Coming and Killing
Cast of Characters
(in order of appearance)
and stage directions

SCENE I

Setting: The stage is divided into two sections connected by a door. The larger section, stage center and right, is a living room. The smaller section, stage left, is a porch. The connecting door is seen by us edge on when it is open, as it is when the curtain rises.

The living room has expensive furnishings that display the benefit of an interior decorator's eye. The couch, upstage center, faces us. A matching loveseat, perpendicular to the couch, is upstage right. The leather is not stretched tight over the cushions. Its slackness suggests its softness. It would probably be comfortable but it is pristine as if rarely used. A glass topped coffee table completes a "conversation grouping." We see two objects on the table, a phone and a heavy-looking lamp, the sort that would serve as a blunt instrument.

The couch, loveseat and carpet are all done in muted colors. Overall, the setting conveys the feeling that the room is designed to make an impression, and that comfort is, at most, of secondary importance.

Beyond the porch we can make out a window of the neighboring building. A curtain is drawn halfway across that window and we see a person peeking out from its edge. She is almost completely hidden behind that curtain, so we can see only her right eye protruding beyond that edge.

At curtain-up we see a couple standing just inside the open door. Outside, on the porch, another person stands nearby, but well away from the door, giving some space to the couple at the doorway.

Crumpet: Bichon Frisé. Family pet. The breed is known to be high maintenance, requiring not only daily grooming, but near-constant attention. From Crumpet's appearance we infer that there has been no skimping on her grooming. She is blindingly white, as if bleached. Her snowy white fleece sets off her coal-black eyes and pink tongue. She is often mistaken for a toy when she is stationary, but is rarely stationary, always demanding attention and usually getting it from Calista, the woman of the household.

Calista Menteuse: The woman of the household. When the curtain rises, she is at the door, facing the porch. We take in her clothes, makeup, nails, hairdo, and the hints of the first round of plastic surgery. From these much can be inferred about her, including a certainty that it is not she who bathes the dog.

She is wearing a polychrome silk lounging outfit bright enough so that she stands out against the muted background of the furniture, but tasteful enough to support her denial of "flashy" in the slinging of neighborhood mud.

Calista is a product of Grosse Pointe, the Detroit suburb once the domain of the royalty of the car industry and still one of the most notable gathering places for Midwestern mansions. This is, as it was in Calista's youth, on the Shore (one of the few local place names for which the final e does not look like a misspelling). Just as the homeless seek homes, those northwest of the Shore struggle to move south and east.

Calista is not a child of the Shore, but of the strugglers. She was, to be sure, denied very little, attending one of the local independent K-12 special schools where she got to meet different ideas and people that she would not encounter later in life.

Calista's mother was halfway through a third marriage during Calista's formative years and contributed to Calista's upbringing mostly with her checkbook.

Pines do not grow from acorns, and Calista patterned her life after that of her mother, a pattern, in fact, that goes back to Calista's grandmother, and possibly further. Calista's own pattern-following was blocked by the nonperformance of her ovaries. She has to fill the maternal void in her life with a needy, troublesome dog.

At curtain-up she is embracing a man we assume is her husband. Her posture, leaning away from the man, shows a lack of enthusiasm for the embrace. Calista's right (downstage) eyelash is falling off, giving her an excuse to turn away from the man to keep hold of the eyelash. Crumpet, meanwhile, is trying to wedge herself between Calista and the man. Her nonstop contralto barking is disturbing to Calista, but much more to the man.

Manfred "Manny" Menteuse: Calista's husband, a Pharma Executive. He is wearing an expensive business suit, and is standing in the open doorway, facing into the living room (facing stage right). By his left foot (hence downstage) is a leather overnight bag with leather belting. It is cream colored except for a dark irregular spot. We correctly see that as a wet spot and understand that it may be the work of Crumpet. The setting tells us he is about to leave on a business trip and is being sent off by his wife with a reluctant goodbye kiss.

Manny and his family describe each other with different animal metaphors. To him they are as poor as church mice; to them he is the black sheep. He left college with a degree in business and grades he does not mention on job applications. His strength is the smoke that is found around mirrors, and a conveniently creative memory for the details of agreements.

His approach to business needs symbols of success. Who, after all, wants to trust a big pharmaceutical contract to a Corolla driver? He needs the wife equivalent of a Mercedes 500 series and sees Calista as the right vehicle. Performance is not the criterion for the choice. What matters, as with the living room furniture, is the impression.

He appears unconcerned that she is all but avoiding the kiss but he is nervous about other things, directing alternating glances at a gold wristwatch and at Crumpet. The dog is moving toward Manny's left foot, and Manny is moving the foot to push Crumpet away. The movement of Manny's foot, and his expression, suggest to us that Manny's actions would be more severe if Calista weren't there.

Reuben Ortega: Taxi driver, medium height, somewhat overweight. Born in El Salvador, he crossed the Rio Grande from Matamoros Mexico to Brownsville, Texas where his cousin Ramón and Ramón's wife Lucia had been poor but happy for six years. Reuben lived in Ramón's basement and worked, poor and not very happy, at a janitorial job in a local high school. He left the job and the town after a little more than a year when Ramón discovered that Reuben's relationship with Lucia had progressed too far past cousin-in-law. Lucia later gave birth to a daughter that Reuben has never seen. He is scrimping so that he can return to Brownsville, claim his daughter, and resettle in South America. He knows that a smile helps his tips, but he is also willing to interpret rules and laws loosely, to do favors that are not strictly legal to earn extra unreported income, to reduce the time before he can again hold his daughter.

At curtain-up, Reuben is standing on the porch, almost invisible stage left. He is slightly downstage from Manny. We can see a small portion of the green and white checkered fender of his cab.

Wanting to be helpful he moves forward to take Manny's small suitcase but stops when he sees the wet spot on the suitcase and sees Crumpet jockeying for position at the couple's feet.

Margaret Aitken: 74-year-old retired widow. She takes ownership pride in the neighborhood and is not of a fan of the Menteuse family. Her health is typical for a woman her age, which means she is a consumer of many pills and biologics, and knows that Manny's company is being investigated by the Department of Justice for fraudulent activities, including a conspiracy to fix the price of a drug she is required to take but can ill afford.

Peeking out from behind her window curtain, extreme stage left, she is following what is happening on the porch and for the moment is staring at Reuben who is moving toward Manny's suitcase. Throughout the play we can see no more than Margaret's right eye, extending slightly beyond the edge of the window curtain.

She takes pleasure in the thought of justice catching up with Manny, in him getting what he deserves. She tells herself that this is the reason for her surveillance at the window, but she was at her window-curtain post long before the Department of Justice started sniffing Manny's footprints.

Ethan Báthory: Calista's yoga instructor and lover. Early thirties, slightly over six feet tall, trim, athletic body. Wearing designer jeans and a tight-fitting tee shirt that shows off his physique. The tee shirt is light yellow with the words "Wanna Asana?" in large mauve letters. His earring has a small icon of the Hindu goddess Parvati with exaggerated female attributes.

Ethan grew up in Mogyoród, a few miles northeast of Budapest. Blessed with natural strength and coordination he excelled at several sports, but not enough to make a living as a professional athlete. Also blessed with good looks Ethan followed a different path and found his niche at Szexi Hölgy (Sexy Lady), a Budapest fitness center catering to women who do not admit to middle age. The owner, László, saw the value of Ethan to his business, but Ethan would not remain at the salary László could afford, so László created the Kovács Institute of Physical Culture, and awarded Ethan, the only Institute employee, the title of Instruction Supervisor.

With this authority Ethan scheduled private sessions at hourly rates befitting his professional stature. His cut and, even more, the tips, were enough for Ethan to drive an Audi sports car. László knew that Ethan's services went beyond ab crunches but said nothing until the husband of one of the

Szexi Hölgy clients brought the extra services to László's attention. The husband was well placed in the Budapest criminal network, so László promised to deal with the matter immediately and appropriately. To avoid what the husband might have considered appropriate, László told Ethan to get out of Hungary immediately. Always the obedient employee, Ethan lowered his profile which rose up again only months later in the Brookline neighborhood of Boston.

Very soon after Manny departs, Ethan appears stage right on the apron of the stage, just forward of the proscenium line. He is standing, holding a phone to his ear with his left (upstage) hand. With his right hand he is playing, demonstrating considerable skill, with a yo-yo. His eyes wander and we see only sparse motions of his mouth indicating his occasional participation in the conversation.

Calista, in her living room downstage center, is also on the phone, so we know that it is she with whom Ethan is talking. She looks around furtively and speaks quietly. Though we cannot hear what she is saying, we can see that she is agitated. She is doing all the talking and is becoming annoyed and showing anger, while Ethan continues to be distracted, paying more attention to the yo-yo than to the phone.

Sofía Krypsins: Personal assistant to Manny. Late twenties, five foot three, exotic looks, olive skin, large dark eyes made just short of cartoonish by overdone eyeliner. She wears noticeable and dramatic scarlet red lipstick that threatens to stain her sheer gauzy white nightgown.

Sofía grew up in Corinth, a small city in the Peloponnese region of Greece, a city with rich history, great natural beauty, stop-and-go industry, and the excitement of frequent major earthquakes. It was not the trembling of the earth that made her move on, but the absence of opportunities for an energetic ambitious young woman. Her yearning took her first to a landing on the upward stairway of her life: an au pair position in Massachusetts. By the age of twenty-one she was fluent in English, but intentionally maintained an accent after being told that it added a garnish of sexiness to her exotic looks. She next worked as a waitress and a barista while hoping to meet the right people and applying for jobs that might take her to the economic and social level she craved.

Manny himself interviewed her when one of her applications came to his company. She had applied to be a pharmaceutical sales associate, a job for which she was spectacularly unqualified, but Manny saw potential and hired her as his personal assistant.

She appears at the same time as Báthory. Like Báthory she is forward of the proscenium line, but on the opposite side of the stage, extreme stage left. She is seated in an upholstered chair. Near her feet is a champagne bottle in a hammered aluminum chilling bucket, with two flutes alongside. In her right (upstage) hand she holds a phone. With her left hand she plays with the champagne bottle, initially turning it whimsically in the bucket.

On the porch we see Manny also holding a phone, as Reuben stands by impatiently.

We can hear neither Manny nor Sofía, but from the pattern—who is speaking at any moment, and who is not—we know that the phone conversation is between the two of them. Much can be inferred from their facial expressions and body language. Sofía shows annoyance evolving into fury. Manny starts calmly but is soon rolling his eyes.

The lights fade as Scene I ends. Curtain down.

SCENE II

Walker Woodley: Courier/lawyer. Less than medium height, maybe 5 foot 7, pale skin with reddish patches. His brown hair has reached its sell-by date and he is combing lacy wisps of what remains from the fringe on one side over the shiny pate to the opposite fringe in the classic combover.

He wears a rumpled dark gray suit and has not taken pains to carefully tuck in his shirt; an edge hangs out over the front of his belt. He is not fat but will be within two years when he blows out the candles on his fiftieth birthday cake.

Walker's arrival at the porch is preceded by the screech of brakes and the roar of a car engine being abused, as if the driver it is not the car's owner and is using the abuse to release barely suppressed aggression.

Walker appears on the porch holding a manila envelope the size of an official document. We can read the very large letters DOJ on the envelope. As he pounds on the door, he calls out "Federal Agent, Department of Justice."

We infer from his expression and the abrupt way he moves that he is in a disagreeable mood. Perhaps a fight with the boss, either at home or at the office. Perhaps just the feistiness of short men. The causes, in fact, go deeper, and back further.

He applied to law school for three successive years, and in so doing developed some skill at applying, so that he was eventually admitted. The second step was loans, and the third step was getting through the courses. The thought of the looming loans was motivational, and he graduated on time to discover that there was a fourth step: getting a position in a law firm. When this step turned out to be the hardest he resigned himself to working for the government and wondering whether he would have the longevity to pay off the loans.

Standing on the porch, Walker thinks about the applications, the loans, the courses, and the outcome: pounding on doors to deliver a subpoena. These thoughts fuel pounding with more force than we might think him capable of.

As he pounds on the door, we see the scene in the living room: Calista holding Crumpet and petting her to keep her quiet while Ethan, now in the Menteuse living room, lies on the couch scrolling through screens on his phone. He glances at the door from time to time, annoyed at the pounding, but otherwise paying little attention.

Woodley disappears from the porch. We hear distant knocking after which the right eye of Margaret Aitken disappears from the edge of the window curtain. We hear Woodley's voice in the distance again shouting "Federal Agent." More loud knocking follows.

We hear a taxicab pull up and can see the green and white checkerboard of Reuben Ortega's fender.

Mumbled voices are heard offstage from the stage left wing. Manny appears on the porch, glances to his right (upstage) aware of and worried by the knocking. He stealthily opens the front door with his key and enters. To avoid the noise of the door closing, he leaves it slightly ajar.

A very few seconds afterward, there is a sound of a car engine being overrevved and the screech of tires. The light in the living room, once supplied by the table lamp, suddenly goes out and the living room is in total darkness.

Andy Steward: Amazon delivery driver. Early-twenties, medium height, medium weight, medium complexion, with the expression, manner and motion of someone always rushing.

Andy did well enough in his first year of community college. It allowed him to live at home, which was good for saving money, but the living at home rubbed like a forgotten label in his Jockey shorts. The baby in the family, he got along reasonably well with his parents, well enough for them to be honest with him. They had seen his two younger sisters through college and were looking forward to reclaiming their lives when Andy turned 18.

A lazier teen would have absorbed the guilt and the friction, but Andy was not absorbent. He took into account that a year off from college, a year away from Mom and Pop, would help him know what he wanted from life. Already he had learned that it wasn't delivering packages while his boss timed him, but he had picked his path for the year and he was going to tread it.

We hear him taking two steps at a time up to the porch before appearing in front of the door with a small cardboard box. He sees that the door is slightly open so reaches out to close it but hesitates when he hears loud crying. He glances at his watch, starts to walk away, turns back, cautiously pushes the door wider and lights the scene with the flashlight in his phone, then switches on the overhead light.

Ethel Firestone: 911 operator who answers the call from Andy. Mid-fifties, gray hair cut short, matronly figure. She is wearing a dark gray wool skirt and a not quite matching well-worn cardigan. There is a bronze medal pinned to the cardigan, too small for us to read.

Ethel is diligent and effective in taking 911 calls. The center of her life and that of her partner Frank, ten years her senior, is Lucy, their daughter. Lucy, now 20, went through the typical stages of the parent-offspring relationship, stages that oversimply to always right/always wrong/who?

The four years of the always-wrong phase were the most difficult of Ethel's life. Recovering from jousting with their own impossible teenagers, Ethel's friends insisted that Lucy was really quite possible. Lucy never acted out with razor blades. (Though it should be noted that both Frank and Ethel used electric shavers in an abundance of caution.) Lucy never brought home a Fonzie; she graduated in the top third of her high school class; she had not been pregnant even once.

More than Lucy, Ethel was the problem. Lucy was Ethel's only child, but was also her only anything. Ethel had no hobbies. She rarely went to the meetings of the garden club she had been nagged into joining. Before there was Lucy there were books, but now a book would sit in her lap always open to the same page. She would read a few lines then look up in case the sound at the door might be Lucy. Worse, it might be the police with terrible news.

There was, after all, the auto accident. Lucy's friend Pamela lost control of the car when a tire blew. The car went off the road into a ditch leaving Pamela unconscious. Lucy's leg was broken but she put it in perspective. She called 911 and within a reasonable time found herself in a hospital emergency room.

Lucy called Ethel the first time she could be truthful in saying everything is under control. Ethel arrived in a time inconsistent with traffic laws to scowl at the emergency room physician. The doctor didn't seem to take Lucy's condition very seriously, saying things like "imple, closed fracture." Ethel was deeply offended by the physician's attitude and subsequently sent a letter to the hospital administration. But at the time Ethel tried to appear calm to avoid scaring Lucy.

When Lucy moved away from home, Ethel felt an urge to connect to her somehow. Though it made little sense, she did this by volunteering to be a 911 operator. As a way of showing her devotion to Lucy she does the 911 job very well, winning several operator-of-the-year brass medals for the region.

Ethel appears forward of the proscenium line, in front of the left stage wing. She sits in front of a small switchboard and wears earphones. We cannot hear what she is saying. From the pattern of their speech we infer that Ethel is talking to Andy

SCENE III

Jessie Huntsman: Rookie cop. Six foot one, sandy hair, barely discernible mustache the same color as his face, late twenties. A body that suggests he is not getting good value from his gym membership, a sucking in of his belly that suggests he intends to do better.

For three years Jesse worked putting up aluminum siding. It was a mystery to him why he was so much slower than Gustavo and Grimaldo, the other men working in the business owned by his uncle Jack. Jesse knew the other two must be cheating but could not pin down just how. The blood that had been thicker than water thinned when Uncle Jack had a fight with Jessie's father about hockey. Jack pulled in Grimaldo's cousin and pushed out Jesse.

The timing was good for entering the Police Academy. The recruiter let Jessie try on a uniform and the Batman belt in front of a full-length mirror. Jesse signed up on the spot and soon was at the Academy. He loved learning about handcuffs and other paraphernalia. They brought a smile and memories of the plastic police toys when he was nine. The heft of the real tools was in a sense a sign that he had grown up.

He had no smile for the classroom sessions in which he learned, or at least was shown, a skimpy summary of city ordinances, criminal law, and police codes. As in any profession, practical jokes were the gauntlet to be run by the new guy. On his second day in a patrol car, the radio importantly shouted "Code 10-54B. Car 27, proceed to the intersection of Bates and Mass Ave."

Jessie's partner could sense the question mark and said "10-54B, a zombie's blocking traffic." One of the older patrolmen had a very different outlook. He thought about Jessie out in public with firearms and wanted to minimize the danger that posed to the people of the city. He explained to Jesse that he would eventually learn the ordinances, laws, and codes from hearing them repeated often, like a child learning a language.

Jesse's real problem becomes interaction with people. The balance of being skeptical/friendly and suspicious/pushy. He looks at Andy, taking comfort in the fact that he exceeds Andy by four inches and forty pounds. At first he glances at Andy the way an insecure bully would look at the new freshman entering the schoolyard. Then he thinks about hidden weapons and martial arts. It is impossible to know these days. Best to be careful.

Jessie is uncertain about what posture and facial expression are appropriate and changes both frequently, paying close attention to the reactions of the others.

He feels like an impostor. He is an impostor. Can they tell? Do they feel the same way, feel that they are impostors? He can't tell. They might just be better at hiding it. He felt this way when he started with aluminum siding. The impostor feeling went away after a few months, despite the expressions of Gustavo and Grimaldo when they looked at Jesse's work.

Lavonnie Baston: Boston police sergeant. Early 50s. Dark skin. Five foot six. No-nonsense solid build. Permanent scowl. She has been in the Department twenty-eight years and is vested in the retirement system.

Her parents rose from the poverty of government housing. They thought of themselves, with justification, as a middle-class Black family that escaped the barriers of racism and, more important, of the structural barrier: not having a node on the network of it's-who-ya-know. They didn't fool themselves, didn't tell themselves the playing field was level. In fact, they took pride in making it despite the tilt.

Lavonnie absorbed the family attitude of "yes, but…" The "but" was the unevenness of law enforcement. Lavonnie heard about this often in anecdotes her parents would relate about humiliations they or their friends suffered. The *Geist* of the Baston kith was not to turn a blind eye, but neither to turn joyous backflips over their progress.

For Lavonnie her middle road was to join the Police Force, to make a difference by her own actions and her example.

That was twenty-eight years ago. Both parents are now gone along with most of her idealism and fire. Lavonnie remains someone who would not cut an ethical corner, though she often asks herself whether it's that she's never been offered enough. Her focus is not the past, but what future the past will give her. She will be getting her pension at 80 percent of the three consecutive years at her highest salary.

She keeps a small calculator in the most accessible of her many pockets, so she can redo, just to be sure, the impact on her retirement pay if she works one more year, two more years, one and a half. Her colleagues are amused by this except when she does it at a tense moment, an arrest or a chase. They tolerate the incessant recalculating while on surveillance although they would prefer to be gossiping about their colleagues. She more or less understands that the focus on the money is creeping toward obsession but she may not grasp its root.

Twenty-eight years ago, when she joined the force, grandparents, uncles, and other sages in the extended Baston family agreed that it was a mistake. She could not remember them ever agreeing on anything else, so the imprint on her was profound. At that long ago moment she did not argue, since she herself was unsure. Retiring with a fat bank account would prove that she had made a wise choice. Those whom she could prove wrong had almost all passed but not out of the images in her head.

She spends surprisingly little time and effort thinking about how the money will be spent. Travel? Surely travel. On her own? With a group?

As she did twenty-eight years ago in the retirement decision, she will take the middle road: stay one more year, then maybe think about it. Of course, one more year means a year of being the mentor to someone like Jessie Huntsman. The Department liked giving her Jessie types because she was a natural teacher. She was surprised at her attitude toward Jessie. Was she getting soft, or was it his resemblance to Larry Bird?

Ryan: Nine-year-old nocturnal skateboarder who insists that he must talk to the police. He is wiry and small for his age, though Ryan, for whom wiseass quips are an art form, tells people he is old for his size. When his hair is called dirty blond, he corrects: just dirty. He has the pale skin expected on a creature of the night.

Ryan's unusual ways would win him friends at school from the clique of the unusual, but he has ignored attempts to reach out to him. Ryan is one of those young people anxious to be older, one who acts as if he is.

His parents are both university faculty members who believe that letting Ryan choose his own path is not only best for Ryan's mental health, but for their own schedules. Ryan seems, and in fact *is* happy, so his parents are happy or would be if the university provost were to keel over with a heart attack.

Ryan's path does not go through the school chess club or junior orchestra; it is the solitary path of cruising the neighborhood at night. The skateboard gives Ryan range, but the wheels are noisy on the rough sidewalks. Ryan will occasionally use the quieter surface of the asphalt but does not lose sight of the danger. He takes small chances but is not a fool. More typically he will ride the sidewalk to a location close to a target house, then walk the final short distance.

He has target houses because Ryan's resentment of his youth spawns a curiosity about adulthood. Having become familiar to the neighborhood's dogs and evening strollers, he raises no eyebrows when he sidles up to homes. He has learned which homes are harboring interesting stories, and where the footholds are in the walls of those homes.

Tobias "Tray" Perdu: Boston Police homicide detective. Early 60s. Medium height, gray hair cut very short and receding so that the hair on the sides is isolated as fringes. He is medium short, maybe five foot eight, maybe not. He is often described as "dumpy," and does not object, though he prefers "fat." He is wearing a trench coat, insensitive to the cliché he presents.

He is a "lifer," a cop his whole life. It was to be his whole life from the beginning, a beginning that is displayed on his desk in framed photos of two former partners, both dead now. The largest desk photo shows him with his wife Marianne as a young married couple. Smiling. He often thinks back on the days of that photo and the years after. Like many of his buddies in the Department, devotion to the job competed with devotion to the family. It would have been better if there had been a child, but they learned early on that it wasn't possible for Marianne.

There was Shere, the tabby cat. It didn't help enough. He took a lesson from the marital breakups of his friends on the force, the drinking problems, the depression. He rebalanced, backed off the pull of the job. He would have advanced more quickly in the Department if he had been a fanatic like some of the others, but those others were suffering.

The job doesn't fit a nine-to-five, just-a-job attitude. He lost the taste for it, and the Department gradually moved him away from the action. Marianne died four years ago. There could be no return to the action, nor did it appeal to him. His buddies in the Department, a dwindling lot, notice him often staring at the large photo on his desk and guess that he is wondering "did I do the right thing?" In fact, he never asks himself that question.

Department regs require that major crimes have a detective sign off on the paperwork. Now and then an easy case coincides with a shortage of detectives, and he gets to saddle up. He is in the living room at the start of the third scene. Baston and Huntsman talk to him at intervals. Huntsman, taking no chances, shows professional respect. Baston does also, though with a subtle touch of something more. Or less.

SLIME MOLD

PART 1: AN AMOEBIC MÉNAGE À TROIS
IN THE WILD

At least in conversations among themselves, *Dictyostelium discoideum* enthusiasts, and there are many, use the pet name *Dicty*, and who can blame them, either for the enthusiasm or the simplification? *Dicty* is feisty about rebelling against categorization as if it wants to embarrass biologists. The best-known example of its uniqueness is its lifestyle: Sometimes a single cell, sometimes a wriggling slug, sometimes a lollipop-like stalk with a colorful blob on top.

The fact that they are called social amoebae indicates how difficult it is to resist anthropomorphizing *Dictys*. Research scientists cannot resist, and their papers have titles that suggest sociology more than biology,[1,2] and phrases that are refreshingly colloquial.[3]

We should cut the scientists much slack since *Dictys* themselves keep their slack taut and uncut. *Dictys* are in the bio junk drawer "protist," which means a shrug of the shoulder. They are

---

[1] P. B. Rainey, *Precarious development: The uncertain social life of cellular slime molds* Proc Natl Acad Sci USA. 2015 Feb 23;112(9):2639–2640

[2] D.P. Armstrong *Why don't cellular slime molds cheat?* J Theor Biol. 1984;109(2):271–283.

[3] "…a sure-fire recipe for conflict" Rainey, *ibid.*

eukaryotes, like us, but then the shoulder shrug starts. They are not animals, plants or fungi.

Their failure to qualify for the last category confronts us with a fiction: the tag slime mold is frequently pinned on *D. discoideum.* Slime is a judgment, but mold is a form of fungus, which a *Dicty* isn't. Here we will not be purists with nomenclature. To do so would also create problems for scientists who have been comfortable (to the extent one can be) as mycologists, and—one supposes—would become protistologists and have to explain themselves far too often.[4]

Those who only dabble in *Dicty* lore know about a cyclic lifestyle that makes the caterpillar-chrysalis-butterfly metamorphosis a yawner. Let us break into the cycle at the "vegetative" stage, in which single amoebae cheerfully wallow in decaying leaves while dining on the bacteria that favor such hangouts. All is well until the *Dictys* have overfished (over-germed?) the area, at which point the *Dictys* face starvation. (That's the word in the research papers, starvation, so it's good enough for us.)

At this point the *Dictys* send out signals[5] summoning all nearby *Dictys*, and they aggregate into a single mass of 100,000, give or take, amoebae. There is a bit of variation here, but let's (the word hardly fits) simplify. The aggregation tightens and, from a patty-like shape, figures out how to become a vertical sort of finger. (There is a temptation to muse on the motivation for a vertical finger, but we need to move on.) Following the script, the finger then falls over into a horizontal slug (research paper word).

---

[4] They would not be on their own. There are aggregates: The International Society of Protistologists and affiliated Asian-Pacific, Japanese, Korean, and Chinese groups.

[5] It's a chemical signal called cyclic adenosine monophosphate. You also could have looked this up.

So far, the stage directions are impressive enough and the reader with any sliver of curiosity will wonder about the communication that allows all the tightening, rising up, and falling over. But now is the moment *D. discoideum* blows socks off. (Not a research paper phrase.) The slug, made up of 100,000 individual amoebae writhes forward seeking fresh (perhaps an inappropriate word) feeding grounds of bacteria-rich decaying organic matter. It is worth repeating: 100,000 individuals move forward as a single multicellular entity.[6]

This, of course, is what an army does, but an army is responding to the orders of a commander. The question that anyone would ask is: How is the slug commander chosen? Is one of the 100,000 amoebae destined to be a leader? We won't stop here, because things get yet stranger.[7] When the slug (or its commander?) decides that a good feeding spot has been found and it's time to set up camp, the slug undergoes a change of shape. In this, its "culmination" stage, it sucks in its middle and squeezes out a vertical structure, one very different from the pre-slug finger. This culminating structure consists of a long filament, the "stalk," with a mass of cells, the "spore" at its top, also known—more fancifully—as a fruiting body.

One way or another, bumped by a tiny woodland whatever, a breeze, whatever, the spore is broken open and the huddled masses inside break out to take up life as individual amoebae, and end the cycle where it started.

We must now backpedal to the culmination and do justice to the stalk, a structure composed of cells that—unlike those in the spore—cannot reproduce. A sad fate that has generated many research papers asking, in effect, what's in it for the stalk cells. This

---

[6] I'm not making this up.
[7] Really

has led to those cells being characterized as "altruistic." There is, as always, more to it, involving the question of cell diversity and the role of wandering "loner" amoebae, (very) roughly equivalent to the rōnin of feudal Japan. Obviously there is much to be discussed here, much grist for the protist research mill, but we need to move on since the story gets better, or worse, depending on your taste.

It involves sex. We must try to clear our minds of images, memories, biases, and most of all, of the mistaken certainty that there are two sexes. In the more flexible approach of more flexible biologists, sex is a way of mixing genetic material to evolve new improved creatures. Our image of this mixing involves the number two, often called male and female, so well suited to all the binaries in our lives and cultures: plus and minus, left and right, wrong and right. But in principle any number can play.

Among the *D. discoideum* amoebae the number is three. The scientists[8] who nailed this down called[9] the three sexes, types I, II, and III. The foundational paper[10] states very specifically that the consequence is the existence of three different offspring possibilities, I/II, I/III, and II,III. The authors note, presumably with straight faces, that "…mating and recombination are probably frequent in the wild."[11]

Wild indeed.

---

[8]Bloomfield, G. et al. Sex determination in the social amoeba *Dictyostelium discoideum. Science* 330, 1533–1536 (2010)

[9]In scientific work, it is, of course, important, especially with a subject as ticklish as sex, to maintain professional decorum. Still, one cannot help but regret the lost opportunities in this naming moment.

[10] Bloomfield *et al. ibid.*

[11] J. M. Flowers et al., PLoS Genet. 6, e1001013 (2010).

"Okay, Jean(II), what's so damn important?"

"Jeez, Pat(I), stop flailing your pseudopods. You don't think something that threatens our triangle's important, hmm? Hmmm?"

"Our triangle? Yeah. Sorry. All ears, ha-ha. Send me some vibrations."

"It's about our acute. It's about Blair(III). She's kind of innocent. Crap, you know that. Anyway, I try to watch out for her. She's been—I think the expression is—led astray."

"Get on with it Jean(II); you're always so goddamn mysterious. I always have to drag anything out of you. What the... What do you mean 'led astray'?"

"She's been carrying on with a sleazy Type I. She admitted it to me. Between tears. But there's stuff she didn't know about this particular Type I. Stuff from the past."

"Oh no, no, no! Jean(II), you're not going to tell me that the Type I is that old sleaze Casey(I)."

"Yup, I'm sorry. Yup, that old sleaze, Casey(I)."

"Jean(II) there's gotta be more. Why would Casey(I) go after our sweet innocent Blair(III) unless Casey(I) is one of those sickos who likes despoiling gentle type IIIs."

"I don't think that's it Pat(I). You know that I had a... umm... relationship with Casey(I). It was about two cycles ago, maybe three. Could even be four. Seems like forever. We had a type III in our triangle, Blake(III). It was me as the Type II. That was it, Casey(I), me as the Type II, and little Blake(III).

"Poor Blake(III)... not sure what happened. We think she didn't aggregate quickly enough, never made it to the next step of the cycle. Just dried out. We heard a rumor that she became a loner, wandering around. Maybe looking for types I and II. Start a new triangle. Just a rumor. But no way. Blake(III) just wasn't the sort. Passive. Know what I mean?

"Anyway, Pat(I), that was it for the old triangle. Finito. Sensible cells look for other compatibles for reproduction, but Casey(I) had what some mycologists call 'issues.' "

"What would you call it Jean(II)?"

"Ummm… It's awkward for me to admit this, but Casey(I) may never have gotten over her feelings for me. All along I kind of suspected that. She wasn't playing the game by the rules: no special angles. All apices equal."

Jean(II) stopped. She was having trouble continuing, but she could see that Pat(I) was impatient and needed her to get on with it, to continue her thoughts about Casey(I). Anyway, Pat(I) could guess what was coming.

"I think that Casey(I) never quite accepted the business of losing me. My guess, and it is kind of boastful, is that Casey(I) developed an attitude that if she couldn't have me, she would destroy our triangle. You me and Blair(III)."

"Jeez Jean, where did you get your ideas?"

"Dunno. Call it cellular intuition."

"Cellular intuition is another expression for worthless bull. But there's no guarantee you're wrong, so the question is what do we do now?"

"Ummm… hold on Pat(I). We're not ready for that question. There's more."

"More! What more?"

"Okay. I told ya that Blair(III) told me about Casey (I). Right. It was an admission. Something she was holding inside, and the "more" was the rest that she was holding inside. It's what made Blair(III) need to talk to me."

Jean(II) gulped and finally filled Pat(I) in on the hidden "more."

"Casey(I) told Blair that she had decided to become a stalk cell."

"Jeeez, Jean(II). Sometimes I just think you make stuff up. Does Blair(III) know what that means!?"

"What it means? Yeah, the end of cycling. The end of reproduction. No more aggregation; no more rising finger, no more riding the wriggling slug, no more rising up to be part of the spore. Damn sight yes. She knows what it means."

"You're saying she volunteered to become a stalk cell. Oh, c'mon. No amoeba *volunteers* to be stalk cell."

"Where did you think that stalk cells came from, Pat(I)?"

"Not sure. Punishment? Bad luck in some kind of lottery?"

"Think about it, Pat(I). You ever hear about altruism? Altruistic cells? You know what that means?"

"More or less."

"It means self-sacrifice, Pat(I). It means that the stalk cells have *chosen* to be stalk cells, to opt out of reproduction, to exit the cycling. Chosen, willing. They volunteered!"

"Yeah. Yeah. Whatever. I never thought about it much."

"You should have, 'cause there's yet more, and it's real bad."

"Jeeez, Jean(II), when's the bad gonna stop?"

"This is it, and it's more than enough. Blair(III) tells me that Casey(I) has been working on her to volunteer. She's pretty much ready to do it."

"I can't believe it. Our Blair(III), our acute Blair(III)? Remember when we first got together? Remember that log, sitting through the wet winter, teeming with bacteria. You and I were stuffing ourselves and we bumped into Blair(III). She was so out of it. Knew nothing. We had to teach her everything about the bacteria, about the sex types. Remember? And now, she's choosing to end it? She's going to be a stalk cell! We can't let her, Jean(II). We can't let her.

We need to change her mind. If we can't, we've got to get to Casey(I). Do something to her."

"I hate this Pat(I). I hate this. Why does reproduction have to be so complicated?"

HALF WITTGENSTEIN

He saw her approaching, flexed the cheek muscles that fake a smile, moved the wineglass to free his right hand so that he could extend it to her. She had the graciousness of a slightly southern accent. Maybe North Carolina he thought. Anything south of Philadelphia was the Deep South to him. He kept his eyes on her and his mind elsewhere.

"Benedict. And you are…?"

"Well, a bit flustered, frankly. You were pointed out to me as Dr. Taylor."

Behind gritted teeth Benedict seethed. The woman thought "doctor" meant physician. Physicians! Workmen who cut and guessed. None of them could get through a page of the *Tractatus* without a gun in their back or a thesis committee in their face. He had a practiced routine that he would tailor to the requirement.

"Yes, I'm Dr. Taylor. Again, you are…?"

"Madeleine. Madeleine Nelson. I wonder whether I could trouble you with a question?"

She wasn't really requesting, just introducing the question. Both understood the exchange not to be literal. Benedict hated the artifice of politeness but saved his railing for more important transgressions.

"My son? Eric? He's five? He has dark stains developing on his arms."

"It's not likely that it's serious."

Next step in the Taylor routine: a question to make him seem all-knowing.

"Does Eric ever play outside barefoot?"

Madeleine Nelson thought for a minute, before turning to Taylor, impressed, and said, "Why yes! Yes, he does! Is that the cause."

"Could be. You have a gardener?"

Madeleine stared at Taylor. Was he a wizard? "Umm, yes, yes we do. He comes once a …"

"Very likely you have a kind of grass called Connecticut fescue, and…"

Madeleine's eyes grew wide, "We live in Connecticut!"

"Your son… Eric, was it?" She nodded in the affirmative. "Eric should check with your family physician to be sure that it isn't Yersinia pestis. There used to be a lot of that going around, especially in Europe."

Taylor was referring to the bacterium that brought the black plague in the fourteenth century.

"We went to Europe two months ago!"

"There is no need to panic Mrs. Nelson. It's probably just the grass. The fescue."

Shaken, Madeleine Nelson pulled her husband away from a small cluster of Pakistani visitors to whom he was declaiming on the failings of the new Giants'

quarterback. She quickly thanked the hostess and left.

Benedict Taylor, professor of philosophy at Columbia, the prestigious Upper West Side university, was known for his treatise *Wittgenstein and the Logic of the Soul.* He took pride in the rumor among graduate students that no one had ever read his book. He knew that to be false since he had a cardboard box of letters, some on vellum and in fountain pen, ranting about how wrong Taylor is.

The details made it look as if the ranters had read at least most of the 412-page tome.

His treatment of Madeleine Nelson was more typical than anomalous. Taylor did not suffer fools gladly but, he felt, too frequently and took it as his right, even his duty, to make them also suffer. The suffering fools were almost exclusively the philosophy majors for whom Taylor's course was a requirement. (A wrong of passage, they quipped.)

On this warm April day, he was dealing with a requirement of his own: meeting with the dean, yet another insufferable fool. Taylor was more curious than worried. Secure in his invulnerability, he thanked the Universe and Ludwig Wittgenstein for tenure. The dean had long ago abandoned any hope of getting Taylor to change his ways. He could not assign more teaching to the campus's most despised teacher; he could not assign more committee assignments to a professor who rarely showed up for meetings.

%%%%%%%%

The two billionaire aspirants contemplated the ironic contrast: the enormity of their futures and the smallness and dumpiness of the one-room apartment they rented when they dropped out of NYU. Greg Borch, the short one sitting there on the desk, insisted it was a two-room apartment, since the bathroom was a separate room. The one sitting against the wall is Sean Usenko. His legs straight out, almost reaching the opposite wall. Sean would be six-two when laid flat in a larger room or hung from a hook, but less than five-eleven standing bent over in his usual hacker's hunch.

Sean wore a dark-red T-shirt that nicely set off the acne still with him from the teenage era that ended two years earlier. The shirt bore the name BileDuct, a klezmer rock band that enjoyed a very short few days of fame during a slow music month. On the back of Sean's T-shirt was the list of the five cities of BileDuct's concert tour. He had been in Albany at the right time.

Sean was staring at a catalog he had just picked up. On the ground floor there was a discount electronics storefront that was supplied mostly from car trunks. It was a toy store to Sean, but he rarely bought anything. The furtive proprietors would shush him away with a catalog as a door prize.

From his roost on the desk Greg sat, legs folded. Not lotus, just ankles crossed, knees pointing up. Back straight. Alert. A compact but athletic five foot eight. He enjoyed the height enhancement of desk-sitting as he orated.

"Sean. Are we too late? Is the age of young innovators now the age of young missed-the-boaters?"

Sean sat silent, absorbed in the catalog.

"What should we do, Sean? Pack it in and go back to NYU? Go back to Mom and Pop? Reclaim the childhood room that Mom was going to use for sewing projects? Not me. I want to experience failure if I have to. I want to tell people about our great idea, Sean. Sean! Are you listening?"

"Jeez. 32 terabytes. Half the price of what I paid a year ago. Half! Un-blanking-believable."

Greg dismounted the desk and pulled the catalog away. Sean looked up, a hurt puppy.

"Hey!"

"I'm talking about our future Sean."

"Yeah, yeah. I was listening. Really. Experience failure. Some-thing about a great idea. Ummm. Huh? We have a great idea?"

"We *do* have a great idea. A 16-TB idea Sean?"

"Fantastic. Our worries are over. Gimme the catalog back."

Greg stared at Sean without speaking. Sean hated that.

"You gonna tell me what the idea is that will make us rich?"

Greg held onto the catalog. Sean would have to listen. Sean hated that.

"Okay. Thinking cap on." Greg mimed the actions of fastening a chin strap. He made thinking noises, chanted "Thinking, thinking, thinking."

"Okay, Sean. We gotta be different. Do something so weird that no one else has already thought of it and sucked out all the shekels."

Greg's eyes were closed, but he was smiling. Sean got nervous when he didn't know where Greg was going.

Greg spoke slowly, nervously trying to give the appearance of patience.

"Sean, we need to bring in users who don't go to any other site."

"You mean muggles, dweebs, people who type with less than one finger, who cannot tell which way the cursor will move."

"Off by infinity, Sean. We want people who hire others to move the mouse for them. We want people who are rich. Good if they're smart—better if they only think they're smart. Rich. Stuck-up, pompous—and proud of it. Rich. They are too high above the masses to ever be found on Facebook, Reddit, X. They would die if someone found out. Rich. Let's call them the Digisnobs."

"Cute. And we're interested in them because…?"

"Hey Sean, you know why giraffes dine so well? I'll tell you: They're the only ones who can get the leaves at the top of acacia trees. That's gonna be why we will bank so well. *High* hanging fruit. No one has tried to pick it. Ripe. No. No. Overripe! The Digisnobs will drip money from great heights."

"And they'll flock to our website because…?"

"We'll have content that no one else would watch. It will make our Digisnobs feel special. Lots of other pluses. We won't have any click bait for commoners. Ads only for ultra luxury brands. No distractions. We'll be smooth, neat, clean. Most of all, *special!* Our Digisnobs like being special.

"But catch this. Pay attention, Sean. How does the teenage crap get a jillion users? Herd behavior. We'll have that going for us with a very different herd. The filthy rich."

"And Greg, our special content will be…?"

"Intellectual!"

Greg's smile did not change, and after a long while Sean realized Greg was serious.

"Great, Greg, that'll have 'em come flocking."

"Sean, Sean, Sean, if no one has told you that you lack vision then eight billion people have slipped up. We're not even going to break new ground. Maybe re-break some old ground that has healed. A billion years ago families sat around something called a TV. You know about TV, Sean?"

"Yeah. Cathode ray tube. X-rays spewed all over the living room. Lousy resolution; 525 lines vertical. Jeez, Greg, I couldn't live that way."

"Yeah, and out on the street you might be crushed by a T Rex. The frontier was rough. But pay attention Sean. Cause we're going to learn from the past. There was a TV program. Long time ago. It was in the '50s…"

"1950s?"

"Jeezus, Sean. Yeah, 1950s. Get with it. The 1850s was before the civil war. Think they had TV?"

"Dunno. Wasn't there."

"Anyway, people would win a lot of money, $64,000, more later on. A lot of money back then. They would have to answer questions. It went viral before there was viral. Daily life stopped when the program was streaming; the streets were empty. The people who ran it, "producers," were raking in the dough. And they knew how to keep the users coming. They did everything to make it compelling. They set it up as a competition. They recruited interesting contestants. They cheated to boost the interest. They went too far, fed answers to keep up the competitive tension and to give an edge to the fan favorite. They got caught. They got spanked. By Congress for Christ's sake.

"So Sean, that's what we're gonna do."

"Greg, how we gonna cheat?"

"No, no, not that part. Well, maybe. But for now, here's the Sean question: Can you set up whatever to stream a kind of contest?"

"Paywall?"

"To be determined. Can you set it up either way?"

"Does the Bernoulli effect suck?"

Greg assumed that it did.

%%%%%%%

Benedict Taylor strolled north on Amsterdam Avenue. It was a pleasant day, and it wasn't as if the dean was going to chide him for being the twelve minutes late he was aiming for. He turned west at the main gate north of 116th and walked past the *Le Penseur* statue.

Taylor was quick to heat and slow to cool. In his first year he could not walk by the statue without boiling over. The statue didn't look anything like someone thinking, unless it was a bodybuilder thinking about where he left his keys. Taylor's attempts to share this wit with colleagues fell flat, and by his second year the annoyance died to a simmer. In the current year, his eighteenth, the statue no longer registered on his retinas as he passed it.

He climbed the stairs to the dean's second floor office arriving ten minutes late; he should have slowed down. Melanie told him to go right in with no mention of his tardiness. He had hoped for a polite comment so that he could politely demonstrate his lack of giving a damn.

As he entered, he saw the expensively framed photo of Dean Marvin Martin shaking hands with Dwight Eisenhower and felt the kind of annoyance that the Rodin statue once provoked. The dean rose and the two men shook hands, two opponents well aware of each other's strengths, appointment power and tenure.

"Thank you for coming Benedict." He added, "Perhaps we should have meetings more often," in a tone that said he would welcome it as much as hemorrhoids, or—for that manner—as much as Taylor would.

"I want to start by discussing the health of your department. How many graduate students do you have Benedict? Is the number I have correct? Seven?"

"It depends what you mean by graduate student Dean Martin, but I believe that the official number is, in fact, seven."

"Benedict, I'm sure you realize that the number is too small to sustain a department of eleven faculty members."

Taylor braced for a familiar sermon as the dean continued.

"Of course, Vendler is getting on in years and he's having some medical problems. We expect him to retire at the end of this semester. By the way, Benedict, how is your health."

"*My* health? Excellent. As an example, I just used the stairs rather than the elevator."

"Benedict, we're on the second floor, and the elevator hasn't worked in over a year."

"Principle of the thing, Dean Martin."

"Yes, Benedict, you've always been a man of principle. So…

back to the status of the department. Gottfried will also be retiring soon, maybe end of the year, and Rossi-Bambilla can be farmed out to service courses in other departments. But still."

"Yes, Dean Martin, but still. It is a sign of the cultural and intellectual decline of the times. Reminiscent of Germany shortly before Hitler came to power. I wish I could do something to help."

Taylor's true wish was for an espresso, but the game had to be played.

"I'm glad you said that, Benedict. It turns out that there is something you can do. If you are willing."

Taylor was the fox feeling the sharp jaws of the trap bite into its leg. He wondered whether he would have to gnaw off the leg.

"Anything within reason Dean Martin."

"I'm glad you have that attitude, Benedict. An opportunity has arisen. You might enjoy it. Hard to predict.

"These days young people are not drawn to philosophy. The opportunity I'm speaking of could, I suppose, be called advertising. Catching the eye of the public with how philosophy can be interesting. Even exciting.

"Two young—stay with me here, Benedict—two young entrepreneurs have presented me with a proposal. A show featuring discussions of deeply philosophical questions. A sort of quodlibetal disputation."

The dean hoped that the use of the arcane term would win him points with Taylor, who viewed it as he would a clumsy attempt of a Philistine to quote the Talmud.

"I'll level with you Benedict. They asked me if I had someone to offer—not sure of just how to say this—someone who had a particularly interesting personality, someone who would draw the most users to the show. Naturally, I thought of you."

"Deeply philosophical questions? Aren't such things already

covered by the universe of nonsense available on the net?"

"The web, Benedict. Yes, but that content lacks the human element, a presenter that the user can recognize, agree with, take issue with, or root for."

"And we would discuss 'deeply philosophical questions'?"

"Benedict, you need to meet with the young entrepreneurs to get the answers you want. Are you willing?"

"No commitment, explicit or implied?"

"Correct."

Check.

"Then, why not?" He thought it best not to list the many reasons why not.

"I will have Melanie set up a lunch as soon as possible. Acceptable?"

"Should be interesting."

Checkmate.

%%%%%%%

"Greg. This tie look right? I tied it a coupla times and, I dunno. Don't think this is the way it's supposed to look."

"Jeezus Sean, were you raised by wolves? First off, you shouldn't be using a square knot. The hard part is the ends. The narrow part is supposed to stop just short of the wide part, so it's hidden. Should be easy for you, not so easy for us of the compact genre. I have to tuck the narrow part under the shirt between two buttons or tie it with a grapefruit-size knot.

"More important…You paying attention, Sean? More important is that you not stain the suit. We don't return the suits in good shape, we don't get our money back from Gents Rentals, and we're out a kilobuck, our rent money.

"Pretty soon a thousand'll be sofa change but now is not then. It wasn't easy to get that loan from my parents. Nobel for pleading. *And*, we're going to need all our pennies for lawyers, and setting up the website. Damn good thing you can handle all the tech."

"Tech, sí; suits and ties, nyet. Let's get it over with. Where we goin'?

"West 96th. Block, block and a half, west of the park. We walk."

Taylor and the dean had arrived a few minutes earlier and had chosen an inside table to make conversation possible, though implausible. In the manner of the restaurants in the neighborhood, tables were packed together like atoms in an ionic crystal. To accommodate a new arrival, an earlier arrival had to stand or slide forward the two or three inches between paunch and table. The waitpeople (for some reason more honorific than waiter) had been trained in the choreography.

When Sean's eyes adjusted to the dark room he muttered *sotto voce*, "Bernoulli." Greg responded in the same voce, "Smile as if your life depended on it. Those steak knives are all I would need."

The academic adults stood to make their presence noticeable in the dim light. It wasn't clear who should introduce whom, so fearing dead air Greg grabbed the metaphoric microphone.

"You must be Prof. Benedict Taylor. Pleased to meet you and excited about the future. This is my business partner Sean Usenko."

Damn. Damn. Damn. Greg couldn't remember the dean's first name.

"And, Sean, this is Dean Martin." Greg saw it coming, wiseass Sean's reaction to hearing that, but Greg stopped it with his heel on Sean's toes; the shoes didn't have to be returned. The two older men wondered about Sean's awkward lurch but said nothing.

The waitperson popped the question "Wine?" Remembering

Greg's instructions and heel, Sean skipped the wine to avoid both wiseass remarks and stains. In what Sean thought a sophisticated manner he asked for a Dr. Pepper, without specifying a vintage.

Greg went about creating the impression of confidence, of knowing what he was doing. It was good enough. He repeated what the dean had told Taylor, the basic idea. Greg's answers to Taylor's questions were what he thought Taylor would want to hear.

He was particularly creative when the dean pointed out that the university counsel would have to approve the contract that Taylor would sign governing the new enterprise. Greg would be sure to hire a lawyer who could deal with this, even if the lawyer's pound of flesh would drive Greg to his knees again in front of Mom and Pop.

Dessert was finished. Hands were shaken. The egg of *Challenge of the Minds* (working title) had been fertilized. Sean's suit was stain-free. As the two young men walked west to build up distance from Taylor and the dean, the Universe looked promising.

Under the cover of traffic noise and the separation of a city block, Sean, frankly impressed by Greg's performance, and disoriented out in the real world, said "What now?"

Greg smiled, looked at Sean, and just said. "Now the good guy."

"Greg, whaddaya mean, 'Now the good guy'?"

Greg liked the superior feeling he got by keeping Sean in the dark, but liked more

showing Sean his cleverness. Besides, keeping him in the loop might avoid an awkward slip of the tongue. One could hope.

"Sean, drama. Movies. You need a good guy and a bad guy. The audience has to love the good guy, hate the bad guy. Gets them engaged. It becomes important to them to see the good guy triumph. It can't be too easy. The good guy has to struggle to defeat the bad guy. Professional wrestling's the same. And ya know what's also the same, Sean? Ya know what's the same? Those $64,000 shows from the '50s. Good guys and bad guys. Every story."

"So we've got our good guy?"
Greg sighed only slightly.
"No. Sean! Remember I said, 'Now the good guy'? We've got our bad guy. Taylor. We've got someone dislikeable, but smart. A competitor worthy to clash with the good guy."
"Cool Greg. Who's our good guy."
"Hang in there Sean. We'll be taking a bus to Princeton next week."

%%%%%%%%

Undergraduate Greg had been just good enough with homework. He knew how much it mattered. Not much. Now he was in a new world. It mattered and he had done it, phoning, rummaging, lying, and coming up with Benedict Taylor's opponent, the good guy. She turned out to be a good gal and was an obvious choice.

Prof. Joby Haskin had been born southwest of Boise, Idaho, born of churchgoing folks who, she emphasized in interviews, never failed to support her liberal ideas though they were so very different from their own. Her father died of a heart attack from working far too hard to support a family that was far too large. Joby, the eldest, was caretaker and housemaker when her mother went to work in the mill to bring in enough for the family to eke by. Though the neighbors' lives were also hard they helped out— it was that kind of time and place.

It would have been rude for Joby to mention an infirmity, but the neighbors did notice that Joby's limp, slight when she was 12, had progressed so much by the time she was eighteen that she had to use a walking stick.

A neighbor drove her to the hospital in Boise where she was told that she had congenital nerve damage in her spine. It could have been treated earlier, but not at age 18. She would be in a wheelchair soon and for the rest of her life.

She was not born to complain. She organized the children with the older ones responsible for the younger. The family survived, and more than survived. All six of her siblings went on to live successful lives, and all believed it was due to Joby, her effort and the model she presented of how they should live their lives.

At age 20 Joby sensed that the family was a boat sailing forward on its own, a boat that she no longer needed to captain. It was time to get back to her own learning. She had never stopped reading and with only two months preparation she had no trouble passing the test for high school equivalency. She contacted the administration at the University of Idaho, in Moscow. There would be no barrier to them accepting her, but it was a time before universities made special allowances for disabled students. Her brother Samuel took a leave of absence from his job, and accompanied her to Moscow, some 300 miles north of Boise.

As Samuel hoped and suspected, his sister's intelligence and spirit caught the attention of those whose attention mattered. Special arrangements were made to get her from class to class. She became well known on campus and, in an action that warmed hearts on the cold western border of Idaho, she was chosen as homecoming queen.

A layer down from the student surface was the action of a few idealistic faculty members who wanted to be sure that Joby would get from life what she was putting into it. They called themselves the Jobites.

Her disability made a few courses impossible. In the others she did well, better than well, and in her junior year she started to think about the next step. Without understanding all the details and consequences of a choice, she looked into herself and saw her future. She would focus on the relationship of ethics and politics. Looking through descriptions of the top US departments, she dreamed about Chicago and Yale.

She made the mistake of, or had the good fortune to, mention her dream to one of the Jobites. Two weeks later, Chicago called to discuss financial support for her. The caller, head of administrative services in the Philosophy Department, asked her "Are you able to teach?" She heard, "Are you able to breathe?"

The following September, at the airport, with all of her family and many of her neighbors waving, some crying, she flew off into her future.

The Universe, trying to make up for its shoddy early treatment intervened in her graduate work. Her thesis, *The Relationship of Intent and Agency*, made a splash that washed east as far as New Jersey, and Joby became the youngest member of the Princeton Philosophy Department. The pages of the calendar flipped quickly and with some element of agency, and variable intent, Joby moved through time to become one of the oldest members of the Department.

For Joby, it was the New Jersey version of the University of Idaho. Joby was recognized, greeted and loved as she wheeled across campus in her top-of-the-line electrified wheelchair ("My Ferrari," she called it). Always in her lap was her tabby Hobbes, without whom many Princeton engineering students would not have been aware that Hobbes was the name of an important philosopher. Unlike his seventeenth-century predecessor, feline Hobbes was tolerant of petting, just as the woman on whose lap he lived was tolerant of the views of others.

Princeton professor Joby Haskin was as famous as a philosophy professor could hope, or fear to be. She appeared before congressional committees several times. Left-leaning committee members were aware of her status as darling of the Princeton liberals and counted on her as an ally. But one of the committee members, a former academic, had actually read some of Joby's writing, and was aware that nuance would get in the way of the simple sound bites they sought. They probably got more than they hoped for anyway. Her charm, clarity, and disability won over the committee conservatives, or at least constrained how they treated her.

The query from the dean's office had IMPORTANT in the subject line, so Joby assumed that a congressional committee was going through official channels to request her presence. For Joby, preaching to the dire had too much been there, too much done that, but team player Joby would accept.

The issue turned out to be much more interesting.

"Joby, good to see you."

"Dean Elway, good to be seen. May I call you Walter."

"Yes, that's the name my parents chose. No need to laugh. Yet. Save it for a minute. I'm going to ask you to take part in a streamed and broadcast competition involving philosophy."

"Competition? Women's wheelchair senior division?"

"You can ask the gantse macher behind the scheme."

Gantse macher. Joby softly snorted appreciation for the phrase. In Chicago and Princeton she had picked up much of the patois, denied her in Idaho, phrases crucial for academic sarcasm.

"When do I raise my hand to ask?"

"A few minutes."

Greg and Sean had gone for coffee after their initial meeting with the Princeton dean. Greg's phone, on the table writhed as if needing the bathroom. Greg turned to Sean with a serious look and an attempt to seem confident. He announced, "We're on," and rose from the table. Ten minutes later he was laying it out for Joby.

Joby listened with amusement and interest. Greg made up answers to her questions, covering most issues with "still in progress." But no evasive cover was needed to answer the most important question:

"Who will be my opponent?"

Greg crossed his fingers steadied his voice and spoke the name as if of the devil, "Benedict Taylor."

"Excellent! I've always wanted to meet him."

%%%%%%%

The early life of Benedict Taylor was as different from Joby Haskins' as Newport, Rhode Island from Boise. Taylor came from a loosely knit but tightly strung neighborhood of people whose children were weapons in the neighborhood rivalry for status and were treated as such in their maintenance and emotional bonds.

His parents fortified his value with tutoring and by steering him away from participation in youth sports and social events. The steering required only the lightest touch on the rudder. Benji (as his parents called him) was ill-coordinated and academically brilliant. Why leave a battleground where he prevailed? The neighbors commented on how proud his parents must be of Benedict (as the neighbors called him), mentioning his absence from many battles with the snide deprecation that was an art form in the neighborhood.

His teachers at the prestigious high school noted in their letters of recommendation that Mr. Taylor (as they called him) was exceptional and kept to themselves that he was exceptionally irritating. His peers in the school, in rare agreement, hoped that

Dickhead (as they called him) would be abducted by aliens, perhaps of his species.

Benedict applied only to Harvard, the alma mater of both his parents. He was given the honor of a full scholarship, though his parents were wealthy. The Harvard accountants/admission officers knew they would get more than tuition money from the transaction. The construction of the Taylor wing of the law school three years later, proved them right.

Benedict's subsequent path brought shame. While the other Ivy legacies went into law, medicine, and finance where they could sow inherited millions and harvest billions, Benedict stayed at Harvard for a PhD in philosophy. "PhD," the letters were bitter in the mouths of Lawrence and Justine Taylor. "MD," "Esq." or "Partner" were the sweet tastes of their hopes. Kids these days! They stayed indoors most of the time to avoid neighbors' smirks.

Benedict rarely got back to Newport after tenure. His was now the world of the intellect, not Gatsbian materialism. He and the Toms and Daisys had no understanding or respect for the other's world. Benedict's description of his provenance always included a claim that he had no jealousy of the mansions and marinas of his native coastal showcase.

The peers who had scorned him, before the college wind scattered the Newport seeds, rarely mentioned him except to ask, before a sip on the second single malt, if he's so smart why isn't he rich?

Now Benedict could show the Yahoos. He would surely prevail in an intellectual joust and would be a figure of admiration among the few in Newport whose barnacle-encrusted minds had not rusted shut. He knew the aging rich/not-smarts would begrudge him recognition but he didn't mind at all. Still, he wanted the philosophy competition to be a hit, and—more than anything else—this depended on whom he would face in the digital colosseum.

Greg had not mentioned specific names for fear that Benedict would sour on the project if they did not sign their first choice. He told Benedict that the decision would be made in two weeks. That was three weeks ago, so Benedict turned over in his mind whether calling Greg would display an unattractive impatience.

While his mind was turning the phone rang and displayed BORCH.

"Prof. Taylor?"

"Yes, this is Taylor. And my phone claims that you are Greg Borch. If so, I infer that you are calling with news about the opponent you propose."

Benedict was rushing past the preliminary pleasantries, anxious to get to a name. He had become emotionally invested in refusing imagined invitations that would follow from the ignorant armies who clashed by yacht size, so the name he would hear would be of great importance.

"Yes. Prof. Taylor, we have consulted with…"

"Greg! The chase. Cut to it!"

"Yessir. You will be matching philosophical wits with Joby Haskins of Princeton."

Benedict's heart beat a happy medieval tune. He had never met Haskins but knew she was a popularizer of philosophy, someone who would appeal to a commoner.

He considered her a lightweight. In the format that Greg had promised him she would be facing a heavyweight, Benedict Taylor. He treated himself to a celebratory dinner in his favorite restaurant and left an unusually generous 12% tip.

%%%%%%%

Greg was snapping at Sean so much that Sean noticed and presented a brief request. "Chill, man."

Sean understood there was no going back, but from where? He was thumbing through the O'Reilly book *Learning the bash shell* and wondering, as he did every few weeks, whether he should switch from C shell.

He said, "So, Greg. Fill me in," and he tried to not to glance at the book.

Greg filled in with exaggerated clarity, making a statement as a sequence of well separated words.

"I hired a lawyer. Expensive, but a must have. We signed a 45-page document. You signed it but possibly forgot."

Sean remembered something about signing something but only remembered that it was long.

"Remember—no, never mind—we had long discussions about format, and about how to pick a panel that would generate the topics and judge the responses. No doubt you remember. Just in case: We stayed away from the Ivies and picked three postdocs. Chicago, Stanford, Duke. They would be paid what, for a philosopher, was a large sum."

"Sean, I'm sure you remember our stroke of luck with publicity."

Just to be sure, and to give himself a chuckle, Greg spelled it out. The Pulitzer-founded Columbia School may be the best journalism school in the world. More important, its graduates believe it to be and are bonded with the elitism and fatalism of Green Berets who survived the same battle. Most of them remembered "Bent Dick Taylor." They networked and shared the memories of the ethics course that Taylor taught until the dean bowed to perhaps hyperbolic threats. When they heard about the clash of the philosophers, they tittered at the thought of revenge served cold.

It often appeared that the "show"—for ultimately that's what it was—would never happen, but appearances were wrong. The dust settled, the Sunday night arrived, and at 9 p.m. Eastern, a tasteful logo appeared announcing the first episode of *Challenge of the Minds.*

A honey-voiced announcer introduced the principals with short biographies accompanied by stills from their childhoods and careers. He announced that while profs Haskins and Taylor moved to positions on stage he hoped users would enjoy a brief description of the luxury watches funding the first segment, pointing out that both the professors chose to wear them. After a tasteful ad, mostly images and classical music, the announcer returned. Greeted the two professors with a serious nod and posed the question, "Will the day ever come on which robots appreciate art?"

He turned to Joby and with a nod let her know she was on.

MULTIPLE TRACKS

Not only is a good prank harmless, but, like a good story, it reveals an essential truth that would otherwise be hidden.——Mac Barnett

"Yes Elena, I know the spoons should be facing the center. That way the water will hit the concave side. It's what the dishwasher engineers would want. Who are we do disappoint them."

"Oh God, Rodney. Why do you have to mock me about everything? You were the one who insisted we put things in the dishwasher the best way. Remember?"

"The accused is guilty and will not seek mercy by recalling how the fair Elena would let spoons face the same way and stick together."

The paired spoons in those early days reminded Rodney of young lovers nestled against each other. It made him smile. It was a long ago. Seven years.

There was silence, not even the sound of clanging dishes as Rodney finished filling the machine, carefully arranging the dishes so they all would fit. They had built up on the counter for almost two days.

"It's Albany this time, right?"

Rodney nodded his head and smiled. The smile was pointless since he avoided looking in her direction.

"If you worked as a salesman maybe you wouldn't have to travel so much. You used to have a great sense of humor, Rodney. Too silly, sometimes, but still. You could win customers over. That, plus you really understand those SEM things."

"Thank you, Elena. We've been over this. I owe it to the company. They paid a lot to train me. The deal was that I would travel to wherever a repair or adjustment was needed. A deal is a deal, and they pay me well to keep my side of the deal."

"You sound like you loaded sixteen tons. You know 'I owe my soul to the company store.'"

Elena tried to sing the last few words in her lowest register, but it was not nearly low enough. She realized it sounded wrong and let it drop.

"And my part? While you're gallivanting around fun places like Albany and Rochester, I get to stay home."

"Elena, I can't back out of an agreement with the company. And when I'm at home we don't do much anyway."

"We could Rodney, we could. We used to."

"Did we?"

"Anyway, it's only for another two years. Then, if I want, the traveling stops."

As he left the kitchen to finish packing, he thought he heard her say "that might be too late." But it could have been something his mind was saying.

%%%%%%%

Walter boarded the train in Poughkeepsie and looked at the unoccupied seat next to Rodney who answered the question on Walter's face.

"Yes, the seat is available. Please, sit down."

"Thanks. Walter." He wasted no words as he held out his hand.

"Hello Walter. Rod. Getting off in Albany?"

"Sooner. Hudson. Stop before Albany. Probably be the only one getting off."

He was silent for less than a minute.

"Don't live there. Live in Jefferson Heights. Get off at Hudson. Get in my car, drive a mile south and cross at the bridge. Ya know what the bridge is?"

Walter took Rodney's silence as the admission that he did not know but was anxious to be told.

"It's the goddamn Rip Van Winkle bridge. Pretty funny, eh. Expect to see sleeping drivers."

Walter looked at Rodney, disappointed.

"Ya know about Rip Van Winkle? Guy who sleeps twenty years. Wakes up, everything is different."

Rodney allowed a tiny smile to suggest that he had known about this fictional sleeper. Walter seemed to want more.

"A lot of that stuff's real close. Sleepy Hollow lake, maybe two miles. Ichabod Crane schoolhouse coupla miles north on the other side. Some people are really into that kind of thing. Not me, but I like how it pumps up real estate interest.

"I'm in real estate, so I know this stuff. Reason I live in Jeff Heights is I'm a smart son of a bitch. Beautiful scenery, big houses, cheap, and a short drive to Albany. Thirty-five miles. Albany is a sure thing for investing. Got what it takes to be a tech center. Rensselaer right there. Easy to get to Rochester, Utica, Syracuse. I'm the guy who's gonna guide the techies to the housing gems around Albany."

It would have been rude for Rodney not to seem interested and he drew a line short of rude.

"Sounds like you've laid out an interesting future."

"You thinkin' about a sure-thing investment, just look me up."

Walter handed Rodney a business card. Not accepting it would cross the rude line.

"And where you off to Rod. You going to Albany, we could set up to talk about real estate."

"I'll have to do that some other time, Walter. Today I'm going to Rochester."

"Rochester! This train is great for me, Rod. But five hours to Rochester. Drive me crazy. You're on business, right. I mean who would go to Rochester for pleasure, huh."

Walter thought that was funny but saw that Rod was not going to laugh. He wondered if he might have insulted Rochester, insulted Rod. Perhaps Rod lived there. But hell, Rochester *was* boring, so why should he feel bad.

"So, your company too cheap to have you fly, or what? Afraid of flying?"

"I used to fly, but when I was 40 I had a near-death experience flying over the Congo. The Kinshasa Congo. You may not know that there are two nations known as the Congo: The Democratic Republic of the Congo, and the Republic of the Congo?"

"What! How's anyone tell them apart?"

"Mostly, people refer to them by the principal cities, Kinshasa for the Democratic one, and Brazzaville for the plain. That's why I said 'Kinshasa Congo' when I mentioned my experience. The two cities are just a mile apart, opposite sides of the river. Crazy, eh? It's impossible to make this stuff up.

"Anyway, Walter, the reason I don't fly isn't fear. It's an homage to Hanno, my partner for many years in many adventures. Few days after that near-death experience, Hanno took the final step, killed in the crash of a small rickety plane. I'd rather not say more because what we were doing wasn't considered strictly legal."

This had enough of an impact on Walter, that he was silent for almost a minute, as Rodney stared off into space. But a minute was Walter's limit, and he was bothered by a detail in Rodney's story.

"Rod, you say this all happened when you were forty years old?"

"Yes, quite a while back, but you understand that it's hard to forget after you've shared adventures for years with a companion."

"Yeah, but Rod, you look barely over forty now."

"Yes, I know. Most people make that mistake. Some even guess early thirties. Actually, I'll be fifty-eight in April."

"No way, Rod. You're trying to put me on."

With no further words, Rodney took out a thin wallet and removed a driver's license that indicated a birthday fifty-eight years ago.

The conductor passed by them announcing, "Next stop Hudson, ten minutes."

"No shit, Rod. Whaddaya have a painting in your attic that's growing old. Ya know like that old movie."

Rodney smiled at the reference.

"The Picture of Dorian Gray, Walter? No. In my attic I have only rats growing fat.

I stay young by eating the right things."

"Well, hell, Rod. What's the right thing. I gotta get off real soon, but you tell me what to eat, I'll follow your advice. Don't care how bad it tastes."

"It doesn't taste that bad. It's kind of expensive, but not outrageous. You should stay away from lettuce but eat lots of watercress. Your salads should be only tomatoes, onions and watercress."

"Exit here for Hudson."

"That's it Rod? That's all?"

"If we had time, I'd sign an affidavit. Good luck Walter."

%%%%%%%%%%

The heavyset man boarded in Latrobe. He had a florid complexion, not the healthy ruddiness of outdoor activity, but that of too much indoor activity with friends and bartenders. Rodney could tell from his appearance and expression that he was a talker.

Rodney moved his coat and slid to his right to make room for the man. The coat had been covering the hard sided briefcase that held Rodney's tools for adjusting the SEM at UPMC in Pittsburgh. As he dealt with his coat Rodney attached authentic-looking toy handcuffs to the tool case and his left wrist. When the coat was moved the heavy man saw the handcuffs. His expression changed and Rod suspected it wouldn't be long before the man started chatting.

It wasn't long.

"Excuse me. I'm usually not nosy, but the handcuffs caught my eye. Afraid of losing your briefcase?"

The man had a nervous smile to let Rodney know it was a joke. Rodney answered with a perfunctory smile. "Something like that."

They sat for a while. Rodney suspected the silence would not last. It didn't.

"Important documents?"

"No. Actually, tools for my work. I fix things."

Rodney had carefully chosen the word "fix" to let the man come to his own conclusions. This man could be counted on to come to the wrong conclusion if given free rein. Rodney waited, without saying more.

"You're probably wondering why I got on at Latrobe."

Rodney did not respond. It hadn't been a question.

"Didja know that Arnold Palmer and Mr. Rogers—ya know,

the cardigan guy—they were both born in Latrobe? That kind of thing cracks me up. I mean suppose you're asking yourself what kind of town Latrobe is and ya find out its two heroes are Palmer and Rogers. Cracks me up. Ya know what else is like that? Morgantown. Biggest city in West Virginia. What's it like? Well, their famous sons are Sam Huff, the tough-as-nails linebacker for the Giants back in the '50s, and Don Knotts, the nervous skinny guy. Cracks me up."

Rodney maintained a weak smile and said nothing. He knew the man would continue.

"Know what's wrong with air travel?"

They both understood that a response was not expected.

"Ya spend an hour or two in the air to get someplace, but it takes hours to get to the airport then hours to get wherever where ya land, and ya spend an hour in the airport waiting for the plane to leave, then an hour getting your baggage.

"Air travel is the slowest way of transportation anyone's invented. Ya going to Europe, okay, beats swimming. But not for going from Charlotte North Carolina to Pittsburgh. Royal pain in the ass getting anywhere in Pittsburgh from that airport.

"Not me. I'm too smart for that. I take a puddle jumper from Charlotte to Latrobe, then hop on the train, and bada bing, in downtown Pittsburgh an hour later."

Rod maintained his thin smile and lack of engagement. He knew the heavy man would not give up.

"You must do important stuff. Ya know. What with the hand-cuffs, I mean. Ya work for the gummint?"

"In a manner of speaking."

"Hmmm. Manner of speaking. Interesting. Gummint got lots of agencies. CIA, FBI. The biggies. But they're like rabbits. They got lots of baby agencies. Some we never hear about. Kinda secrets. Hush hush. Manner of speaking. Ya maybe in one of those?"

"If it's secret I wouldn't tell you, would I?"

"Yeah, yeah. I get it. Wow."

Rodney thought to himself, for such a fat man he jumps to conclusions pretty well. Rodney was curious about what would come next. He would have to wait a minute or two. The man was framing just the right question.

"So, you fix things. Interesting. Lemme ask something since ya *may* know about this kind of thing. Just guessing. There are rumors that Russia has agents to kill enemies, 'specially foreigners living in Russia. Ya know. Assassinate 'em. Right?"

This was going in the direction Rodney had hoped. It was time for him to start engaging.

"They are not rumors. Those political assassinations are beyond question. We know for certain that some of our diplomats have been killed."

"Okay. So figures that the good guys—us—we also do it. Kill enemies."

"Yes, I suppose it figures."

"That means that the gummint sends out guys—hell, maybe women—to *fix* things."

"Yes, I suppose it does."

"And it would be very hush hush. Wouldn't want anyone to catch on."

"I suppose you're right."

"Wow."

The man sat quietly for a few minutes, thinking about the stories he would tell his friends. Rodney knew what was going on in the man's head. It wouldn't be long before they would be detraining in Pittsburgh. Rodney put the icing on the cake.

"Sir, I don't want to seem nosy but are you meeting anyone at Union Station in Pittsburgh."

The heavy man was off balance and answered in a voice different from the one he had been using.

"Umm… yes. I'm meeting my wife."

"I don't want us to get off the train at the same time. I'm going to hang back when you get off. Let me suggest that you move off the platform, get inside, as quickly as possible."

The florid complexion had turned to pale.

"Is there danger?"

"Oh no, no. Call it an excess of caution."

THE MEADOW

A slight twitch of Bear's finger and the grotesquely muscular KonQuR raised his gun and twisted his face into a blood chilling grimace. KonQuR heeded another finger twitch and the world exploded into a dancefloor of bloody body parts while KonQuR's deep bass laughter boomed through the speakers.

It could have gone on a great deal longer. Bear had taken only three direct hits and was at the ninth level. But the light gray Manhattan afternoon was dissolving into dark gray evening. Bear had been at it since just after lunch, and it wasn't that much of a game anyway. Good graphics, but a derivative work, not all that different from *DeathBlazt III* or the latest *Blood Reaper*.

Bear went toward the kitchen to see what his mother was doing about dinner though he really didn't care. He wasn't in the mood for talking and, after a quick glance, continued past the kitchen door to sink into the quicksand of the living room sofa, grabbing the remote control on his descent. Without great effort he could reach the plate of pistachio nuts so he did. The shells held some interest, but it would be wrong to waste the nuts themselves, what with children starving, so he ate. Each nut gave him two half shells and two opportunities to hit the small brass basket near the other end of the vast sofa. It took great skill and Bear hadn't had a strike in more than a week. But Bear was not one to shrink from such a challenge.

Enid Lofgren emerged from the kitchen and stood patiently, waiting. Bear flicked the two half shells he had just earned and by way of greeting ended the shell flicking. "Bear?" she smiled, "Didn't you go out of the house at all today?" He told the television that he hadn't; he wasn't feeling well. "I'm worried about you, Bear. I'm making an appointment with Dr. Kornberg."

Had Dr. Kornberg possessed instruments sensitive to such things, he might have found that late on the previous day Bear received the news that Artie had been

killed in Afghanistan. This news aside, there was nothing wrong with Bear that hadn't been wrong for a long time.

To the extent that Bear acknowledged his own feelings, he thought back about feeling quite a bit better five years earlier. The computer games then had been crude, though his interest in them was waning; high school took up a big part of his day. His friend Artie had decided to go to Science High, the special science and math high school. He mentioned it to Bear who thought what the hell, I'll go also. Math had been easy for him. He hadn't really been interested in junior high school science, but neither was the teacher. The two friends laughed about Mrs. Praeger's scientific howlers.

From time to time Artie would share something with Bear that he had just learned, the curvature of spacetime, or the way leaves on ferns exhibit mathematical patterns. Math sounded to Bear like the right kind of rule-based stuff, definitive and predictable, like a computer game. He knew that he was good at it, and he didn't know what else to do.

The name on his birth certificate was Burr. This was a respected old Swedish name

and was the name of Bear's respected old Swedish grandfather, who might have felt honored had he not died many years before

Bear was born. But Bear's few friends, and many classmates couldn't very well call him Burr, though no one had ever explained why. Bear was slight of build and slighter of aggressiveness, so the nickname was ironic, as if a pet turtle had been named Speedy, and irony often passed for wit in Bear's crowd of New Yorkers in training. In any case, the name won the contest of what-to-call-Burr that had been going on and off since Bear started school. Those that constituted his circle tried calling him Aaron, after hearing about Aaron Burr in history class. Burberry had a brief run in seventh grade, but lacked monosyllabic punch. One of the ninth-grade horde threw in the suggestion Frosty, and pantomimed shivering while making the sound brrrrrr. The author of that name refused to recognize rejection and, until the high school diaspora, greeted Bear with a shiver. Bear accepted this without complaint since he was basically good-natured or at least nonconfrontational.

Artie had no such identification crisis. He was christened Arturo a few months after Burr was born and no one had a second thought about the diminution to Artie, and hence no one stopped to consider how appropriate the name might be.

Artie and Bear were drawn to each other in school by their shared lack of interests.

Neither had any interest in any aspect of sports. Artie was bemused by, and Bear repelled by most extracurricular school activities. Curricular activities were another thing entirely. Both were gifted with mathematical ability. Bear's was pronounced, while Artie's was his destiny.

In high school the two friends became a threesome with the addition of Sam, who

had to travel an hour each way to get back and forth between his home and the special high school. This commute left him less time than Bear and Artie had to hang out and ponder the meaning of things. But Sam did spare the time to be a participant in the trio's brief moment of senior year fame.

They had the fortune to be together in Mr. Court's class for senior rhetoric and literature. Mr. Court, despite having taught for twenty years, was still an idealist who gently pushed the students to think. Though students at Science High didn't believe that thinking and literature went together, Mr. Court loved working with these kids and showing them that they were wrong. He was the rare example of a happy man.

As he did every year, he required the students to find a book of "significant literary value" and write a five-page paper expressing their own original thoughts about the book, along with clear justification for their thoughts. It was Bear who launched the caper with, "Why don't we make up books."

Sam added a stroke of brilliance, "We'll each do a book in a trilogy we make up, something like *The Lord of the Rings*."

Artie could not resist, suppressed his misgivings, and added a touch in his own style. "It can be the great epic in the mythology of Fluoristan."

The coconspirators, sensing they were onto something, next thickened the plot, trying to stay outside, but close to the bounds of good taste (and hence trying to help Bear distinguish faux literature from faux video game). "Symbols, lots of symbols…" "And messages, something deep…" "Sexual awakening. Swords and scabbards…"

In the end they reported on the three volumes of *The Lake of the Moritori*. In addition to being nonexistent, the trilogy was notable in that there were no references in its 1,234 nonexistent pages (in the English translation from the original Fluoristani) to any lake or to the name "Moritori." This enigma was pointed out by Sam in his report on the first volume, *The Saddle of the Lamm*. Bear deconstructed the second volume, *Descent into the Peak*, and Artie analyzed the climactic final volume, *Horses on Fire*.

In one way this was more work than simply finding some acceptable short novel and developing or faking enough of an opinion to fill five pages. But in another way it turned out to be easier, and certainly more enjoyable, to create as well as analyze. And it made for much crisper analysis. One could start with a few good sentences about clouds as a symbol and then create several excellent examples of how the shading of the clouds mirrored the action of the plot. Artie pushed this technique to the edge with his observation of the twelve distinct examples of juggling by dwarves presaging bad luck, an observation that was indisputable once it was pointed out but might have been missed by a reader less observant than Artie.

Each of the creator-critics referred consistently to the other volumes of the trilogy, and the three injected mock serious literary criticism to the slight extent that their senses of humor would allow. It did not bother the Science High Literary Trio that their reports were transparent fabrications. They would be bothered only if they were not funny, skillful fabrications. Nor did the result bother Mr. Court, who understood that they had learned more from their effort than the students who handed in uninspiring rearrangements of buzz phrases they found on their computers. He required from the boys only a promise that they would read, on their own, a real book, and discuss it among themselves. Mr. Court lived up to the trio's expectations, and they to his. That summer they surprised themselves at how prolonged were their arguments about John Gardner's Grendel.

Science high school hadn't been a bad decision for Bear. He was never going to be another Artie, even if he worked at it. Sam did work at it, and it got Sam to number 47 in the graduating class, not up there with the geniuses, like Artie. While Artie jumped the high academic fences, and Sam plowed through them, Bear grazed his way along the low meadows, going through the fences whenever he noticed an open gate. Bear ended up as 292 in the graduating class of just under 700. Not a whole lot different from forty-seven. His parents' conversations at that time seldom lacked the phrase "top half at Science High." That had been long ago, and his top half glory was long faded. In his parents' social conversation now, Bear made brief and infrequent appearances, and then only in answers.

The path from Science High was narrow and led only to college. Artie would seek his fortune in the West, at Caltech, but Bear didn't even consider applying. Sam was going to Cornell, and Bear made another what the hell decision. In September he would go to Cornell and become an electrical engineer. His engineering career would be based on math, but in engineering he wouldn't be trapped into an academic future. The decision had been in February; with the start of the fall semester safely in the distant future it was hard to take the decision seriously.

That was the last year Bear would be living in New York City and seeing his parents regularly. The realization came as no shock. Since Bear's fifth birthday, when it was clear that Bear would have the capacity to read and write, a first-rate college away from home was a firmly fixed part of his future.

Bear's parents had made no effort to influence Bear's choice of college. They understood that it would have been wrong; they understood better that it would be unsuccessful. But Arne Lofgren was not displeased that his son had chosen Cornell, his own alma mater. Arne did not deceive himself that this fact had been an important element in his son's decision.

September came, that year, promptly at the end of the summer.

Though this was typical of Septembers, Bear seemed surprised that what had once been only some shuffling of paper would now require a shuffling of Bear himself some 200 miles to an unfamiliar and hence uncomfortable town that might be his home for the next four years. He considered backing out, but that would have required much more activity and inconvenience than doing what was expected of him, so he did the expected.

Bear was to spend his first year in the freshman dorms in a double room. On the roommate preference card he had listed first "blonde coed, freckles if possible" but was satisfied with his second choice, Sam Bergman. Having Sam as a touchstone to his previous life made the new life more nearly acceptable. In the few days before classes started they roamed together through the beautiful upstate New York fall, getting oriented in the vast campus and the nearby town.

The first of Artie's infrequent emails arrived soon.

Date: Thurs, 2 Sept 1999 16:23:07 -0700 (PDT)
From: Arturo Campanelli <artcamp@caltech.edu>
To: <blofgren@cornell.edu>,<sbergman2@cornell.edu>
Subject: college studs

dudes

pasadena is like 30 miles from the ocean. its not all beach bunnies in bikinis here. its more like genius nerds in overalls from exotic places like nebraska. for the first time i feel unnerdy with my NYC street smarts. the only other kid from sci hi is yan wang who was 2nd in our class, but ive only seen him a couple of times. let me know whats up with you ivy league elitist snobs.
artie

Classes had started and for a while Bear attended, along with Sam. Their background at an academically tough high school gave them an advantage over most of their classmates. Sam played the ant, using their academic advantage to store up high homework and exam scores. Bear, the grasshopper, faced with no great challenges, faced no challenges at all. He chose to coast.

Sigurd the Victorious walked through the calm meadow on level 1. The elves and gremlins were of no concern. He smote them with his bare fists. They disappeared from the meadow and left no trace. Sigurd was saving his weapons for the unknown dangers that lay ahead, and paid scant attention to the small demons that were an insult to his powers.

Coasting had to come to an end, and Bear ran out of downhill by the end of the first month. Some of his classmates, quick learners out of the classroom, had already packed it in and headed home. Bear wasn't ready for that but neither was he ready to spend more hours studying than sleeping. He was very uncomfortable, and did not like being uncomfortable.

Date: Wed, 06 Oct 1999 01:12:23 -0800 (PST)
From: Arturo Campanelli <artcamp@caltech.edu>
To: <blofgren@cornell.edu>,<sbergman2@cornell.edu>
Subject: tale of two techs

dudes
this is the best of places. it is the worst of places. The professors are research stars but sometimes the teaching sucks. Its like high school. the students learn from each other. the profs impose schedule and fear. it works.
artie

Bear was putting some effort into his non-math courses, and was following the efficient approach he had developed in high school. Reasonable effort gets pretty good grades; the last step up the grade ladder is a large and pointless one. Calculus was another matter. He had done very well in calculus at Science High, and the university course seemed to be covering much the same material, so it would have taken exceptional irresponsibility for Bear to do poorly in the course, but Bear was exceptional.

He viewed Calc as if he were taking English as a second language. He was already fluent. The Calc study time he saved allowed him, though only in principle, to put more time into other courses. When he failed the first Calc exam he reconsidered. He told himself he was rusty and promised himself to get serious about studying. Then he would show them. But he didn't listen to himself.

He discussed with Sam his failure on that first exam, on which Sam had done the third best among all freshmen, but later Bear didn't share with Sam the news of his failure on the second exam. He emailed Artie about that second failure. Maybe the computer seemed like a confessional because Bear couldn't see Artie's face. Or maybe it wasn't the computer; maybe it was Artie. Artie's reaction was what Bear expected: no clichés, and an offer to do whatever he could to help Bear.

Sigurd the Victorious had fallen into the trap. What seemed to be a gentle meadow had been a gradually steepening slope, and ahead lay a precipice. Sigurd turned to climb back up the slope but his armor was heavy and the ground was slippery. He found progress too difficult. The sky was flashing around him. Lightning hit all around him blasting huge pits in the earth on all sides. Demons were visible when the lightning flashed, but drawing his sword might attract the lightning. He saw a cave, a chance to be safe.

At the start of November, Bear had a confrontation with his old enemy, reality. He could still pass the course if he suddenly became very studious. But Bear knew his enemy well. There had to be another way.

Though he saw the irony and tackiness in it, he envied Sam. Sam's family was poor. Not hungry poor, but not in a position to give Sam any money for college. Sam got a very generous scholarship and took out loans. He could have gotten a job on campus, to make money for a few luxuries like movies and beers, but Sam didn't want luxuries, and he wanted to take no chances with his grades. Sleeping eight hours a night would have been taking a chance, so he got by with five hours, to have the extra time to study. He grew a beard, initially to save a few minutes shaving, but began to be proud of this mark of imagined maturity.

Sam may have struggled with sleep deprivation, but he had no struggle with decisions. Sam depended on his scholarship, and the scholarship depended on a cumulative B average. He had nightmares about getting a C minus, probably in freshman composition. Several times a day he would compute what combination of A and B+ grades would be needed to compensate for that C minus.

In Sam's mind there were two futures for him as distinct as good and evil. Failure now was failure forever. Struggle and success now would give him the opportunity for struggle and success later. The ultimate success would be to be a tenured professor, like Bear's father, teaching, getting small grants, publishing papers now and then. Neither of Sam's parents had college degrees, and his father, whom Bear had never met, had not finished high school.

Date: Wed, 3 Nov 1999 01:12:23 -0800 (PST)
From: Arturo Campanelli <artcamp@caltech.edu>
To: <blofgren@cornell.edu>,<sbergman2@cornell.edu>
Subject: bias adjust

dudes
the local fauna: theres one kid with a billy joe bubba accent. Hes from alabama. no really. from alabama. he was telling me about quantum computing. the bastard has already published a paper on it! ive got to adjust my biases.
artie

Bear started turning in his calculus homework, and suspected that with some of the rust removed he would do okay on the third exam. Okay, but not spectacularly. That wasn't going to be good enough. For perhaps the first time he felt about a grade the anxiety he felt when threatened in a computer game.

Date: Mon, 15 Nov 1999 03:07:45 -0800 (PST)
From: Arturo Campanelli <artcamp@caltech.edu>
To: <blofgren@cornell.edu>,<sbergman2@cornell.edu>
Subject: honorarium

dudes
speaking of different: the caltech honor system. everything is really open. you can take exams wherever you want. if there is cheating the students deal with it. there is almost no cheating. jeeez the other kids are so smart i am tempted. but here it just seems wrong. im getting to sort of like this place.
Artie

There was no way out for Sigurd. In the cave of no return he had climbed down the rope of indolence, a rope that could not be ascended. Around him slithered the slimy sea monsters of Asvarth, flicking their tails, and licking their bloodstained teeth. The screen flashed, and speakers crackled as the towering dragon loomed from its deadly plinth, spitting acid fireballs at Sigurd, already relishing the carnage to come. Sigurd reached for his sword, but in his scabbard he found only a dagger. It would take Thor himself to save Sigurd now.

He wondered how Artie would have done in such a situation. Of course, Artie, though not motivated primarily by grades, never let things get completely out of hand. But if Artie had not done anything in the course up to this point, Artie could still pull out a good grade by doing brilliantly on the remaining preliminary exam and on the final.

For the first time, he wished intensely that Artie was nearby. In math and science, Artie was such a superhero that the focus on Artie removed any focus from Bear. Artie, unassuming Artie, was a kind of math superhero who could do the impossible. Bear was not.

It was at around this time, the time of Bear's bleakness, that Sam, by contrast, started believing he would survive the trial by B. He was on his way to A or A+ in almost every class. He was counting on at least a B+ from freshman composition, in which he felt he had neither talent nor (Lake of the Moritori aside) interest. His anxiety attacks, though still frequent, subsided enough for him to talk to Leah in his Russian class. Sam and Leah used the Russian class as an excuse to spend time together and gradually lost the need for excuses. Like Sam, Leah was Jewish. Coming from Buffalo, Leah's provenance was exotic enough to be interesting but not frightening like such terrae incognitae as Alabama and Nebraska. Her Buffalo roots did, however, carry the minor baggage of popular culture. As Bear observed the growing relationship between Sam and Leah, he semi-sang, not apropos of anything in particular, "Buffalo gals won't you put out tonight, put out tonight...?" Sam was only mildly annoyed at this, since he had formed a similar question in his own mind, a question that would take months to progress to his voice.

Bear's envy was less than his surprise at Sam's good fortune (or was it more than fortune?). He regretted that he would not be around to watch the development of the Sam and Leah story, since he, Bear, was about to write a coda to his own story on the third Calc exam. Failing calculus would not, in principle, require that he leave the university, but he saw little point in starting a math-based career with a D grade.

Date: Mon, 29 Nov 1999 8:34:02 -0800 (PST)
From: Arturo Campanelli <artcamp@caltech.edu>
To: <blofgren@cornell.edu>
Subject: burn this message

mr phelps
ok. ill do it, but not your way. a button mic hidden in your ear is ok, but using a webcam for me to see the exam is too easy for a hawk eyed professor to catch. besides its just too ordinary for the knights of the moritori. here's the plan. do what you can do on your own. then call the prof over to ask some dumb question that requires you to read the whole problem out loud. also its not as if i know absolutely everything so send me the name of your text book and the chapters that will be covered on the test. shit. as long as were doing this we might as well do it well.
your accomplice
artie

With Artie in Bear's ear, an ear covered by long hair, Bear was relaxed enough to do very well on his own until he came to the twenty point problem that was meant to remind the students that they didn't really understand calculus. Up went Bear's hand and overcame the professor. "Excuse me sir. In problem 2B, it says 'A plane curve has a unit normal. The derivative of the normal with respect to arc-length has a constant magnitude. Find the type of curve and prove your answer.' What do you mean by 'arc-length'?" The professor sighed, gave a short answer and was pleased to see that it was all Bear needed to turn happily to his paper.

Bear made the rookie mistake of handing in a perfect paper, while none of the others in the class could handle problem 2B. On the final exam Bear artfully injected errors, that kept him from the awkwardness of getting a perfect score, but did not keep him from the still awkward highest grade among all freshman, higher therefore than Sam who was a shameful seventh. The instructor was surprised. He had seen late-semester conversions before, although none so dramatic, so he called Bear into his office for a chance to probe Bear's math. He chose not to focus on the stuff of the course itself but on mathematical ability more generally, and ended up impressed with Bear, suggesting that Bear might consider choosing a math major.

During the long winter break Bear and Artie both went back to the City. They looked at each other almost shyly when they first met at Artie's home. Their imitation of small talk would have fooled almost no one, certainly not Artie's mother, whom almost no one could fool. She knew something was up.

It was only outside in the anonymity of the New York City streets that they could talk freely. "Jeez Artie, we're not Leopold and Loeb. I mean we didn't hurt anyone. Two years after graduation, all those jerks in Calc won't remember anything, and I'll probably be using math every day. Our big crime was like going sixty-five in a fifty-five zone, in a Ferrari, with no other cars around. It was just temporary anyway. I got myself in a hole."

"So it's over? We're not going to continue next semester?"

"Yeah. No. No. I was thinking that we should keep at it just for a while. Otherwise it will look strange that my exam scores suddenly drop."

"Okay, okay. But Bear, old buddy, you've got to do the homework. If they buy the whole package that you suddenly got religion, you've got to do the homework. Promise me that you will do the homework."

"Deal. I'll do the homework, and I'll try to catch up so that we can stop the cheating after the first exam."

It was the first time either of them had spoken the C word.

With his lightly used batteries freshly recharged, Bear returned to school for the spring semester and diligently did the first two math assignments, but the third assignment seemed to him to be full of pointless repetitious drudgery that taught nothing. He was sure that Artie would understand. Skipping those problems demonstrated his superiority. He was sophisticated enough to disdain those pointless problems.

Bear's demonstration the following week was even more sophisticated, since he did none of the problems. He relented for the fifth assignment after an uncharacteristically stern email from Artie, but reverted to sophistication for the sixth. Meanwhile, the math test tag team of Artie and Bear, becoming more cautious, had settled for only a very good grade on the first spring semester exam.

Artie became restive seeing no sign their ongoing misdemeanor was winding down. Bear said they could discuss it when they met in New York for spring break, but that turned out to be too late. Disaster struck during the second spring exam.

Artie had not been practicing safe cheating and was caught in flagrante. One of the others in his student residence house heard his phone call to Artie, and inferred from some of Artie's remarks that help was being given not on a homework assignment, but on an exam.

He first told Artie what he was going to do, then he reported the transgression to the Student Honor Board. Both Artie and the snitch thought that the punishment would be light, since Artie was helping a friend, not helping himself.

At his hearing, the Honor Board asked Artie to reveal the identity of his partner in crime. Artie refused, saying, quite correctly, that the identity was not relevant to Artie's own guilt, and swearing that he had been doing it only to help a friend, not for money, or blackmail, or such circumstance that would darken his actions. Though the Honor Board made a formal criticism of his failure to bring another perpetrator to justice, it was not their job to police cheating at other institutions. It was obvious to everyone, even to Artie, that they felt Artie was doing the honorable thing by keeping the secret.

And the punishment was light: Artie was put on what amounted to ethical probation. His professors were alerted that he had been involved in cheating, and the usual freedoms given to students were to be denied to him. He was to have a graduate student observe him personally during all exams. It was as if he were wearing a scarlet C.

Artie explained all this, or most of it, in an email. Bear's breathing stopped at the first sentence and he scanned until he found the hoped-for assurance that Bear's identity had been protected. He knew of course that Artie's cooperation wouldn't be needed if anyone cared about tracking down the loser that Artie was helping. Bear would just have to wait and see.

The message was not accusatory, but it seemed as if Artie were far away not only in miles. Bear did not know what to say in reply, so rather than risk saying the wrong thing, he said nothing. And heard nothing. When something is put off, it becomes more and more challenging to face it, and more and more unchallenging to put it off further. After two months it became clear how distant the two friends had become when Bear got a telephone call from his own mother. Bear felt uncomfortable talking to her in general, but felt a much different kind of discomfort when she asked, "Artie has quit school and has joined the army. His mother is frantic about this. She said that you and Artie seemed to be up to something during winter break. Do you know anything about this?"

Certainly Bear knew *something* about this, but he had no trouble acting surprised, since he was, and claimed complete, rather than partial ignorance. For the first time in many years his mother had information that was important to him, and he broke a long tradition by speaking to her more than was absolutely necessary. He also called her Mom. He usually didn't call her anything. "Mom, do you know anything else about this?'

"A little more. Mrs. Campanelli says that Artie joined with a guarantee that he could be in the Army Corps of Engineers, if Artie passes some tests. And of course Artie has never failed a test in his life. He gets to build things for people."

Date: Thurs, 08 Sept 2000 07:45:59 -0500 (CDT)
From: Arturo Campanelli <acampanellip@mil.gov>
To: <blofgren@cornell.edu>,<sbergman2@cornell.edu>
Subject: off 2C world

dudes
boot camp isnt anything like what you imagine. its worse. bear-it was kind of like being surrounded by mrss praegers. they didn't really understand the technical stuff that they were teaching us but now we have to pay attention. the mrss praegers have

become officers and we cant get away with the crap we did in
mid school.

but really honestly guys it isnt that bad. im clearly way ahead of
these dudes in the technical stuff but they know lots of stuff that
may save my life. what i really like is the way things here are
really focused on getting stuff done. its like universities take creative people and make organizations to stop them from creating.

the military takes ordinary people and just gets stuff done.
i cant tell you where im going. that seems really silly to me, and
the rule will probably change next week, but ive learned to accept
the militarys silliness. following rules is how to get stuff done
even if the rules are stupid. the rules in academics are stupid too.
maybe stupider.

when i joined i was promised a chance to use my abilities and to
help people, and it looks as if they are going tokeep that promise.
im going to have lots of interesting stories to tell when i get back.
you guys will just have stories of exams and hangovers.

Eat your hearts out.
Specialist A. Campanelli

*Sigurd stopped for a moment on the ninth level, ragged and bloodied. The
screen was dark. He knew not what monsters lay around him or ahead. He
would have to move cautiously. Or perhaps stay where he was and wait.*

NITA

I was on my way back to my job. A little grumpy, maybe more than a little. The thing wrong with being a cop, which is what I am, is that the job is more interesting than the time off. Interesting but tense. I didn't want the time off, but no choice. Wasn't just the Swedish focus on work-life balance. I'd have to remain an unbalanced outlier Swede. It was about the job tension. They thought I needed a break from it. They, the HR automatons immune to tension, immune to my arguments.

The first two days away I couldn't clear my mind of the cases I had turned over to Nita. So getting away was counterproductive. The tension was worse because now I couldn't do anything about those cases. By the third day I was starting to forget the details of the cases, starting to feel relaxed. It should have ended there, on the third day, but it didn't. And as tension exited, boredom entered.

A lot of cops use alcohol to deal with the tension. I saw what it did to a colleague who'd been a good cop and I wouldn't let it do that to me. I never had a drinking problem and was not going to let two weeks off drive me to one. When I found myself reaching for a drink I reasoned I would be better off on a motorcycle than on a couch within reach of akvavit. I had ridden a bike in my early 20s and was pretty sure the skill would come back quickly. It did. I rented a 750cc Honda, a helmet and leathers, and rode to Oslo and back, stopping at interesting looking inns along the way. The bike was a comfortable cruiser. But it was a motorcycle. It insisted on attention or it would hurt you. I forgot about the files, about what Nita would be doing with my unfinished cases. It was a relatively warm late September, but not too warm and the chill was invigorating. The ride turned out to be one of my good ideas.

The Oslo trip ended three days ago, and I returned to police life yesterday. It gave me two days. Just enough time for tension to start building up and for some grumpiness to return. And it was in evidence yesterday as I walked on the Polhemsgatan from my apartment, past the mostly gray buildings. Police headquarters in Kungsholmen took a cautious step from gray to a sandy salmon color. My mood was matched by the air and the sky. The clock said morning, but it was always late afternoon in Stockholm's November.

The large room we smirkingly called the cop shop was divided by partitions into democratically Swedishly equal-size work spaces. Each with the same computer workstation, the same fluorescent desk lamp. Each shining a circle of light down on each gray-topped desk created a scene of spotlights on a broad stage. The stage of the human tragicomedy I once said to myself. But only once. It was too poetic for the shoveling of the detritus of wasted lives that was most of our work.

I was the boss, the Kriminalkommissarie, the Detective Chief Inspector, so I rated a desk in a small separate room attached to the cop shop. Nita, filling my chair, as well as my duties, was in that room. I put off meeting with her for a few minutes as I acclimated.

I exchanged nods of greeting with Nils, short for Bjorn-Nils Erikson. A running joke was that Nils was short for a cop. He was very good-natured but the joke got tiresome. As the boss, the DCI, I told everyone to stop the joking. I was Rik, short for Carl-Eric

Nilsson. Not short for a cop, but short tempered. Especially yesterday.

Nils, who handled the Department's administrative details had a desk apart. Someone quicker to take offense might have taken it, but Nils was too popular to be ostracized. Even Lucas the dour, though he tried, could not complain about him. Nils' location minimized the disturbance of the frequent visits of his cop colleagues seeking bureaucratic balm. His competence in providing it was part of his popularity. Nils was also a keen diagnostician with an old dog's sensitivity to mood.

"You want coffee Chief?"

It wasn't really a question, and he didn't listen for an answer but went to the coffee machine to fetch my medicine. This once I'd let him do the fetching. Medicated, I approached my office and its occupant. She saw me through the glass door and said come in before I knocked.

As I entered she stood up as if she were a man acknowledging a woman's entrance. It was slightly awkward, but there was always awkwardness looming when we were together. It wasn't serious enough for either of us to admit that it affected our work. We exchanged a brief perfunctory greeting before getting down to that work.

The trace of timidity in Nita's voice was only for me. She was confident in her conversations with other officers. A minor part of this was that she called me "Chief Nilsson." The others called me "Chief." Some called me "Rik" but looked nervous when they did. I was okay being Rik. I didn't worry how they addressed me to my face. I didn't even much care what they called me behind my back.

"Unless you object, Chief Nilsson, I'm going to put on hold the progress reports on the cases that remained open when you left, except to tell you that three have been closed, including the

Bjorklund case. There's something new you should know about…"

"You closed the Bjorklund case? Impressive!"

Nita flushed. She was uncomfortable with compliments from me. I think it was only from me.

"We just got lucky with Bjorklund. Let me tell you about the new case. A murder. Day before yesterday. The body was found in the bushes in Tantolunden park. That's a big park in…"

"In Södermalm. I know the place, Nita. You and I had a picnic there once."

I had almost learned to tolerate Nita's denial of our past relationship as if denying mention could erase it. I was willing to go along with that. Mentioning the picnic was a slip up. I think. Maybe not. It's not as if I know what I'm doing.

"Anyway, the body was identified immediately. Hugo Hoffmann. He was accused of sexually assaulting a child, an 11-year old girl, mutilating and murdering her. The evidence…"

"Usch! An 11-year old kid… Jesus. Sorry, Nita.

"Solid evidence, but not enough for a judge. We started following Hoffmann. Thought we were being discreet, but not enough, I guess. He complained and we were forced to back off. Turned out to be fatal for Hoffmann. Kind of ironic.

"Hoffmann's body was in dense foliage on the southeast side of the park. He was a user and a seller of drugs, so it could have been a drug deal gone bad. But we favor the idea of revenge by a relative of the 11-year-old victim. Didn't have to be a relative, of course, could have been someone who just knew the kid, and couldn't stomach the failure of justice. Anyway, the body was found by a couple, Carl and Astrid Hansen, looking for a place to be alone. Finding a body probably cooled the lovers' ardor."

"All details in the folder?"

"Right, Chief Nilsson. It's yours now. I'm gonna take my stapler and coffee cup and return to the big room."

Anita-Karen Gustaffson, "Nita," had come to Stockholm thirty-one years ago at age 10. Even at that age she wanted to be a police detective, and nothing stopped her.

She was a Kriminalinspektör, a Detective Inspector, the rank just below mine.

Unless she did something uncharacteristic she would move into my job—she'd become the DCI—when I moved up or out.

She was physically attractive, but that wasn't it. What did me in was the closeness of working together on crimes. The drawing together when we faced the things people could do to each other. I think we had trouble being alone in the ugliness of that world we dealt with and we took shelter in each other. So it was the job that led to the bed. Or that's the excuse I use to myself. God how I hate to be unoriginal. I hoped that before long Nita would get over it. She would or she wouldn't. Either way, it was tolerable and life would go on.

I grabbed another cup of coffee while Nita was moving her stuff. In my office I forced myself to hold off on looking at the new case as I quickly skimmed over the status of the still open old cases, checking whether any immediate action was needed. I didn't want to ask Nita. I was on my third cup when I opened the new folder.

It started with a review of the case against Hoffman. I couldn't take issue with the conclusions implied in the file. I would have bet my pension that he had killed that poor girl. He was seen with her a few hours before she disappeared. On the walls of Hoffmann's apartment the investigators found photos of chubby blonde preteen girls; one of them was clearly identified as the girl who disappeared. Most frustrating was the blood found on a shirt in

Hoffman's room. It was matched to the blood of the 11-year old girl, but the shirt had been removed without a warrant and the judge ruled it out. The usual bullshit about chain of custody.

I understood that there were rules; there had to be. The girl, too young to be anything but innocent, had been abused, had suffered terribly at the end of that short innocent life. But I understood. I understood.

What I needed to focus on was not Hoffmann the psycho murder, but Hoffmann the victim. Nita had made a start in the investigation. I would follow up right after lunch, but lunch would be an important self-indulgence. Therapy with Bent. I'd last met with him a week before my no-choice vacation, so it'd been three weeks since the last meeting. I'd gone longer before, but it was a hassle for him to drive in from Vallentuna. He said he'd be in Kungsholmen today. I took it as a hint from the heavens.

A lot of cops have another cop they can bitch to, can bounce ideas off. Someone who'll tell them they've been screwed when they have been but also tell them to suck it up when they're just pouting and whining. Bent was my go-to. That made me feel special because Bent was special. He was in his second year of law school when St. Sherlock, the patron saint of police detectives, whispered in his ear. It wasn't that Bent found law school boring. Okay, it *was* that he found law school boring. Anyway, he became a cop who had some legal background, great commonsense intelligence, and proficiency with a headlock. A great cop.

I always thought that Bent—great cop that he was—really missed his true calling but I wasn't sure what that would be. Maybe a philosophy professor. He was so damn smart. You know how some smart people make you feel small and stupid? He was the opposite. After listening to him you felt grateful to be living on a planet that had Bent.

My good luck was that he took me under his wing right off when I arrived in the Department. My bad luck was that the wing carried him off to retirement five years later. He left in a goodbye party knee-deep in booze and tears, a party that still brings a dreamy look to those who were in the Department at the time. Seems like a long time ago because it was. I continued to use him as my go-to therapist and minister. At least once a week until he moved out to Vallentuna with poor Mimi. (Standing joke tradition in the Department: wife Mimi was always "poor Mimi.") I couldn't help but smile when I saw Bent sitting at the bar.

"Hey Rik, I ordered this beer for you. I heard about your Easy Rider jaunt to Oslo. I gotta get you drinking again."

"Good to see you Bent. Better than good. Great. I've missed you. Enough idle chatter. I feel a need to talk. You feel a need to listen?"

"Sounds bad. Sit down and talk."

I told him about the Hoffmann case and my confused mixture of feelings about how Hoffmann slithered free of the cops who now have to break their butts looking for the hero who killed him. The case was new, but the feelings weren't.

"Question is Bent, what's our goal here, really? Justice? What the hell is justice? If a rule about chain of custody lets slime like Hoffmann laugh at us, that's not justice. No way. No way, Bent."

"Not an original thought Rik."

"I know the argument Bent. Rules *are* justice. We're in a game, and games have rules. Cops start making their own decisions, and the rules stop meaning anything. People start thinking that every-thing's an opinion. Can't have law and order without order.

"I know, I know all that, but damn it, I can't get myself excited about catching the guy who killed Hoffmann, except to ask him whether Hoffmann suffered, cause it couldn'a been enough. That warped walking slime should…"

My voice trailed off. I couldn't find words strong enough.

"Hey Rik, I get it. Every thinking cop goes through that struggle."

"Did you, Bent? Did *you*? And if you did what side of the fence did you land on? Rules or justice?"

Bent was quiet for a long time. I could tell that he was remembering something and trying to decide what to tell me.

"Yeah, well, this may not be what you want, but it may be what you need. Not sure whether it will help or hurt for you to know that there have been other Hoffmann cases, will probably be more. Maybe it'll help to know what cops have done.

"It was something that happened around thirty years ago. I was new in the Department. Everyone was talking about a sexual assault torture and murder in Tórshavn. You know where that is?"

"Yeah. Faroe Islands. Capital, I think. Second in command in the Department, Anita-Karen Gustaffson, was born there. I remember this from the paperwork when she joined. Came over as a youngster, age 10. Meant she was a Danish citizen. Applied for Swedish citizenship when she turned 18."

"She came on long after I was out to pasture."

"She missed a hell of a party Bent."

"Stop it Rik. You don't want to see a senior citizen cry. Anyway, I never met her. Interesting city Tórshavn. Holds the record for the least sunlight of any city in the world. Makes you wonder whether that accounts for insane acts."

"What I'm wondering is whether you're gonna tell me about the Tórshavn murder."

"Stop wondering. I'm gonna tell you. It might be important for you to hear it right. Thirty years ago. Some things are impossible to forget, but forgetting details is easy. When I get home I'm gonna look at the files I copied before leaving the Department. (Not quite allowed. You're not going to rat me out about this, right?) I'll call you and give it to you with no maybe's and more-or-less's."

When I got back to the Department I wanted to grab a driver. It woulda made sense for it to be Nita, but sense wasn't the only consideration. I looked at the board with the list of which officer was doing what.

"Andersson, grab your driving gloves. I'm gonna trust you to drive me to Tantolunden."

"Picnic, Chief?"

He knew damn well why we were going there. I don't like being a hard-ass, but it just wasn't a time for jokes. I gave him an icy stare but it hit the back of his head.

I was following my habit in investigations: check out first those things that are going to disappear first. In the Hoffman case it was the murder scene. Hence the drive. I wanted a driver so on the drive I could read a section I had skipped over in the file. It was from the part covering the murder of the little girl, the thoughts of the forensic psychologist. Hoffman fit the profile of a killer of a child. Not a member of the family. Signs that he lived in a fantasy world hidden from his neighbors. A suggestion in his background that as a child he would have admired an adult who was brutal and violent.

We parked in the lot closest to where the body was found, the Ringvägen lot, probably the lot that the murderer used if he drove. The yellow tape was still up identifying the murder scene a short distance into the nearby bushes. The file in my hand had notations that corresponded to numbers on evidence flags at the site, so we could see where the body had been found. A few meters away, there was a spot identified in the file as where one of the Hansens had vomited. I knew from experience not to assume that it was

Astrid. I looked again in the file, looked at the picture of Hoffmann's body. Just a body, not very different from a sleeping person. Still, an unexpected murdered body curdles the stomach of someone spared such sights in daily life.

I couldn't keep myself from thinking about the contrast, maybe I wanted to think about it, about the pictures in the file of Hoffmann the murderer, to think about what the last hours must have been like for that poor 11-year old girl. The pictures showed the small chubby body with a face that looked angelic despite her last minutes. In a few years she would have started thinking about boys, about her figure. She might have joined a gym. Spent a lot of time in front of a mirror. Had days of tears and days of laughter. Hoffman stole all that from her. I felt my jaw tighten and felt—actually heard—the sound of my breathing becoming rapid. I gave myself a moment to regain the objectivity I needed.

In the file Nita had noted some nearby scraping of the soil, as if the murderer had started to dig a grave. Seeing that for myself was high priority, the reason for the visit to the site. I concurred with Nita's suggestion that the marks were made by a shovel. It meant that the murderer was going to bury the body, perhaps to delay the discovery and let evidence grow cold. He must have taken off when he heard the Hansens approaching. This was very important. It meant that we had an exact time for the murder. We could search for evidence of vehicles moving around Tantolunden right at that time. More important, the shovel might be key evidence. These days the forensic elves could pull fingerprints off cotton balls.

Nita hadn't missed that and had started the search. In the Ringvägen parking lot we were only 150 meters, no more, from the scene. If the murderer had a shovel he must have come by car. Nita's notes said that there was an attendant on duty at the car hire company in the lot. He reported that a man rushed out of the woods at a time within minutes after the Hansens stumbled on the body. The attendant noticed because the man acted agitated. He slowed down and regained his composure when he realized the attendant was watching him.

Nita asked the right question, "Was the man carrying a shovel?" The attendant gave the wrong answer, "No."

He must have dropped the shovel as he hurried toward the lot. We had the timing tight enough that he couldn't have stopped to do a good job of hiding it. He probably would have thrown it into the densest bushes he passed as he ran to the lot. That brought us to the big question. When the police presence started to thin out did he come back to recover the shovel? Good chance that he didn't. The shovel could still be there.

Nita was a half-step ahead of me. Maybe a whole step. After filing the initial report and doing the necessary initial paper shuffling, she went back on her own to search the bushes between the crime scene and the Ringvägen lot.

Why hadn't she taken a few officers with her? Why hadn't she searched the bushes immediately when she was first there, instead of having to return? It wasn't smart, and Nita is smart. The light was getting dim and Andersson was clearing his throat more than his throat needed. I took the hint. There would be no point in doing my own search for the shovel.

We headed back to the cop shop. Only a 15-minute drive even in the traffic at that time, but for those minutes my eyebrows were knitted above a cynical squint.

Andersson, usually insensitive, was aware of it. "Something bothering you Chief." "No," I lied.

Back in my apartment I turned on music. I just wanted background. Like many, Swedes and not, I had overdosed on ABBA. I put in a CD by Anyone's Daughter. Music with a narration of the Hermann Hesse poem *Piktors Verwandlungen*. I don't speak German and didn't much like the music. When I turned it to low volume it served the purpose.

I would have gone to a restaurant. My first day back on the job and I was tired, but I was expecting that call from Bent, and didn't want to be in public when it came. I found something in the freezer from the pre-time off era and irradiated it. I should have gone out. Bent's call didn't come until 10 p.m.

"Sorry it's so late Rik. Mimi said I sleep on the couch if I don't take her to see that new movie *Blade Runner*."

"Worth watching?"

"Not if you're a cop. Too much was unrealistic. I know it's science fiction, but for me too much fiction, not enough science. But let's get to what I want to tell you about Tórshavn in 1988. It'll be worth the wait.

"Starts in the early eighties, could be late seventies. We're in Murmansk, a Russian oblast, kinda means province. Actually in a small—coupla thousand pop—town Safonovo, around three kilometers from the port of Murmansk. Here we find the devil incarnate. Chinggis, no last name but it's an adopted name anyway. Chinggis Khan's is an alternate tag for the national hero of Mongolia, Genghis Khan. We don't know what he was doing earlier or how he ended up in Safonovo. How could we? We didn't even know the bastard's real name before he landed there. But I can fill you in with some background to his arrival in the Faroe Islands.

"Chinggis was a poster of what a Mongol male should look like: leathery skin, broad face, low cheekbones, slanted narrow—very narrow - eyes, medium height but powerful build. He shows up with a Sami girl that the neighbors think might be maybe 15 years old. You know about the Samis, right? Skin and hair so fair they look albino or translucent. Makes 'em look younger than they really are, so his girlfriend might have only looked fifteen. But maybe she was fifteen. So don't jump to any conclusions.

"Safonovo was a really small place, coupla thousand, like I said. Just one magistrate to tell people to obey the laws and hope they do. Like everyone else, he is terrified of Chinggis. So Chinggis lives there for a couple of years with no hassles. It's assumed that Safonovo is a base of operations. Chinggis disappears for days, sometimes weeks. It's a rough part of the world, and times are rough. No one bothers asking him details.

"He finally goes too far. People hear screams and the nearest neighbor, peering through binoculars while he cowers behind a shuttered window, sees Chinggis stabbing his Sami girlfriend then dragging her body into the woods. The magistrate gets a message to the head of the Council of Deputies in Murmansk. Chinggis is not afraid of much, but he is afraid of the Red Army; they're just as brutal as he is. Chinggis must have had an informant because a few hours before a squad of Red Army soldiers arrives in Safonovo, Chinggis takes the train south from Murmansk. We figured he had either been stealing jewelry, or converted his loot to jewelry, so that he could easily hide it and use it to support himself for the next couple of years.

"The Russians told us they think he's looking for a place like Murmansk. Far north, enough people, but not too many. He settles on the Faroe Islands and makes his entrance to Tórshavn around 1985. He's got phony papers. The cops are very suspicious, but Chinggis keeps a low profile. He buys a house in a village called Hvitanes maybe four kilometers from the center of Tórshavn. Houses are far apart there. Just what he wants.

"He plays it smart for a year or two, worried that Red Army intelligence is still searching for him. But around that time the

Soviet Union is coming apart. Chinggis figures they have more to deal with than a lawless Mongul, so he stops playing it so smart. Starts taking chances.

"He had distinctive looks of course, so he's always spotted when he goes into town and the police are notified. He drives an everyman car. Gray, dusty. But his license number is on a slip of paper in most homes.

"Time wears away diligence. As the months pass the residents put away binoculars and rifles. Chinggis knew it was coming and was biding his time, temporarily suppressing an obsession he could not control for long. He drives around the coastal roads looking for preteen girls hiking home after school. One day in the spring of 1988 he gets lucky, and a 10-year-old girl gets tragically unlucky.

"We don't know just how he gets her into the car. There are some standard tricks, usually faking an injury and needing some kind of help. That was a favorite of the American serial killer Ted Bundy. Of course, Bundy preyed on older girls and didn't look scary like Chinggis. But Chinggis might have been a good con man, glib enough to fool a 10-year-old. Of course, he could have just jumped out of the car and grabbed her. We'll never know. They're both dead.

"When she's reported missing some in the town immediately suspect Chinggis. Others, led by the minister, say it isn't fair to blame him simply because he's different. Of course, he isn't simply just different.

"By the next morning, the police have reports of Chinggis's car on the coastal road the day before, around the time school let out. It was the road the 10-year old would have taken. There are several stretches on the road that cannot be seen from any of the houses. The police look at those stretches and find one with signs of a struggle. Turned up turf, that kind of thing. They comb the area for anything that might be evidence. Nothing.

"The police question Chinggis, whose alibi is that he was at home at the time. He lives alone, so no one can confirm. They get a warrant to search his home and take his car into the police lab. Nothing.

"Around three days later, there's a gruesome break in the case. Dogs were used to sniff around Hvitanes. They find a gravesite. The little girl's body is in it. She had been abused. The killer must have been harboring some terrible psychological pain. He wanted her to suffer. She would have survived for many minutes as the killer used his knife to let blood drain from her. A tree branch had been forced into her anus. Hard-ass cops became sick at the site. One of the cops prayed to Jesus that she died quickly.

"Near the grave there are boot prints. Many were brushed over as if a makeshift broom was used, a branch with some leaves. But the killer was sloppy. There are still a few boot prints. The cops make a cast and it turns out to be a match to Chinggis's boots.

"A squad of cops with automatic weapons knock on Chinggis' door. He knows he'd lose a firefight and goes along peacefully, protesting his innocence.

"Tórshavn's a small city, more like a small town. Lots of people knew the 10-year-old. The story about the condition of the corpse was leaked by some of the cops. They needed to talk; couldn't get over the trauma, the images. Some fool leaked the discovery of the boot prints, and the police had to barricade the station against a crowd coming to pull Chinggis out and hang him. Probably worse.

"The whole character of the city changed. From a safe friendly haven to a terrified population that locked doors and did not go out at night. You might think the tragedy would make people come together. In some ways it did; in other ways the opposite effect. Maybe they lost their belief there was good in people.

"At Chinggis' arraignment the prosecutor asks the judge to deny release on bail. The judge says that the evidence isn't overwhelming. Besides escaping from Tórshavn is impossible with the airport and piers all on alert and the whole damn city watching, staring, and hating. So Chinggis is set free to await the start of his trial, weeks in the future. But the trial never happens.

"Chinggis's body is found next to the gravesite where the poor little girl was found. His head had been bashed in with a bat or a club. Aside from that he isn't mutilated. The police report no evidence at the scene, and no leads.

"When Chinggis was released at the arraignment, those outside the inner circle wondered why Chinggis's safety was not considered. No one would answer their questions and they learned not to ask any more. They were satisfied when the search for Chinggis' murderer was dropped after a few days.

"The townspeople of Tórshavn looked at each other with conspiratorial glances. They said nothing, but they knew. Not the details, but they knew."

Bent's long story was over and I was silent. I wasn't stupid enough to ask Bent why he wanted me to hear the story. I knew. There was very little to say but I broke the almost sacred silence with a question. I asked it without my usual veneer of smartass.

"Bent, how do you know all these details?"

"Ah Rik, always asking insightful questions. I got these details from Ragnar Kjærbæk. Hell of a name, no? He's of my vintage. Now living on memories but was head of the small Tórshavn Department in '88. He was not only willing to talk about it back then. I sensed he wanted to."

I understood that Kjærbæk would have sought the same Bent-therapy I did. I said my second round of thank you and goodbye, and softly pressed the button to turn the phone off. I knew I would have trouble sleeping.

The next day I tucked Bent's story into the back of my mind. I had things to take care of. A couple of everyday cop things, and a big thing: Nita going back to the scene to look for the shovel. Why? Asking Nita was not the right step.

I didn't want a driver. There was no telling where this investigation was going and I didn't want to constrain possibilities. I checked out a car with no police ID. It was a Saab 900, not too old. Could be fun if it was the turbo. This is how I am. Facing pain I turn to trivia. It wasn't a turbo. Life is unfair

Traffic was very light so the drive itself took about the same time as adjusting the seat and the mirrors in the Saab. I went over the Västerbron, the West Bridge, turned left on Hornsgatan, turned right on Ringvägan, and 300 meters down the road was in the parking lot.

I parked in one of the car rental slots. That would bring out the attendant, which is what I was after. As he walked toward me I suppressed a smile. He stopped, unsure whether to continue. It was not the attendant who had seen the killer rush out of the bushes. But it was an attendant I knew well. When he recognized me, he stopped.

"It's okay, Marko. If you did anything wrong I don't know about it."

I had arrested Marko Jovanović two years ago. He had emigrated from the boneyard of Yugoslavia. Neighbors killing each other in grotesque violence, Srebenica, Kosovo. I was appalled but could not look away. It made me read. I read about the Tutsi genocide in Rwanda, La Violencia in Colombia. The horrors wrought by the Nazis was not an anomaly. Evil was built into people. They could blind themselves. Not only turn off empathy but turn off recognition of the humanness of others. If I could have laughed I would have laughed at the absurdity that God made man in his image. Man was an abomination. Did that mean that God was an abomination?

I had to report to work every day so I had pushed Yugoslavia and the rest to the back of my mind. It was always there. From time to time it would emerge.

As a refugee Marko was having a hard time finding work. He was skilled at disabling car alarms and removing expensive parts. I had a sense that he would keep his nose clean if he had a job and was given a chance. Yes, I am too soft to be a cop. Don't tell anyone. I got Marko a suspended sentence and called on the manager of a car rental company who believed in human salvage operations. Another softy.

"Detective Nilsson. Good to see you. You here check my nose clean?"

He had remembered my warning to him.

"No, I would have heard if you were sticking it in dirty places. I'm here for a very different reason. And Marko, you are lucky. You may be able to help me."

"For you Detective Nilsson, any help you want would make me very happy."

"Let me see if I can make you happy, Marko. Were you on duty yesterday afternoon?"

"Give minute. Yesterday long time ago."

I was astounded that Marko retained or regrew a sense of humor. I think it's one of the things that softened me toward him even more than usual with a petty criminal. Some things in the essence of a person are almost impossible to quash. With Marko it was his innately clean nose and sense of humor. It was also his refusal in speaking to use articles, unnecessary garnishes absent in Slavic languages.

"Yesterday just after lunch to about six in evening. But little business here; nothing suspicious Detective Nilsson."

"That's okay. What I want to know is whether you noticed a police car parking in the lot."

"Yes. Yes. Police car. Woman driver. She park very close to bushes. She park with driver door on side of bushes, so only I see enough to know she cop and woman."

"What did she do after parking?"

"She go into bushes. Disappear. Come back later maybe twenty minutes, maybe half hour."

"Was she carrying anything when she returned?"

"Ah Detective Nilsson. That right question. I think—not sure, but think—she throws something in back seat before she gets into driver seat. Then takes off on Ringvägen road."

"Thank you Marko. I'll let you get back to your kiosk."

"I help?"

"Yes. Be happy."

As I drove back to Kungsholmen, my mind was not on the road. The Saab was more tolerant than a motorcycle, so I survived. I dropped it off in the basement car park and pondered. I wanted to talk to Ragnar Kjærbæk. I could call Bent and ask for contact info, but the fewer people who knew what I was doing, the better. I went to my office. I noted the remaining trace of Nita's perfume or shampoo or whatever and had no reaction. I asked my workstation to find Ragnar's phone number. I wasn't going to be paranoid enough to do the search behind some digital veil. But I did walk outside to make the call on my mobile.

I told Kjærbæk who I was and that Bent had related the story of the 1988 child assault in Tórshavn. He perked up when I mentioned Bent, then perked back down when I mentioned the assault.

"How can I help you Chief Inspector Nilsson?"

"It's a background question, really. I'd like to know, or at least to hear your take on the long-term aftereffects in the Tórshavn community. Back in '88 you told Bent that the murder changed the whole feeling in the city. How long did that seem to last?"

"In my opinion, it's winding down, but not yet completely gone. Some people had to leave to escape the mood and the memory. Others lived with it and many still live with it. People who arrived after '88 sensed the depression and paranoia. Some even joined in; most did not. The impact was worst on the kids, especially young girls at the time of the assault and murder. Counseling was arranged. Some of the kids could stuff it in the back of their minds, maybe time bombs. Some couldn't even do that. That's also pretty much true in some measure of everyone who was Tórshavn in '88. It takes more than a generation for new attitudes. Moses knew that, eh?"

"Thank you Chief Kjærbæk. That has been very useful."

We were a few days into November. The sun was low. I started walking south on Polhmesgatan. I could have crossed the street and walked in the Kronobergsparken, but being near the bushes would have the wrong effect. I needed to make a decision. I wanted to have a blank mind. Not think, just feel.

THE RED DIGITS

yles Harrison squinted, confused at the fuzzy red digits. His eyes focused as the mist of sleep dimmed and he understood the numbers on his alarm clock were mixing with his fading dream. A recurring dream: The meeting around the conference table. Vice President Alaric ("Big Al") Sanzenbacher was embarrassing Myles in front of the company's Executive Committee.

Big Al died three months ago, but not in Myles's dreams. Sometimes the dream came for no reason; last night there was a reason. Myles was going to present his strategic proposal for the company. For the first time, without Sanzenbacher there to torment him, he wouldn't stutter and sweat. A chance to show the board what he could do, and the timing was perfect.

Myles was sure there were demographic shifts starting that other real estate companies had overlooked. It was a chance for his company to get a jump on the competition. There would be a risk, but the traditional real estate business was ebbing. It was innovate or disappear. He would be valued for his strategic vision. The board would understand that it is better to be creative, to take chances. To be passive was an express ticket to failure. He would use those words.

He had time to go over his presentation a last time, maybe twice, before catching the train downtown. His excitement fought the warmth of the quilt on the unseasonably chilly March morning; the quilt came in second.

At 6:30 a.m. Kathy was usually already out of bed and downstairs brewing coffee. He assumed she was, so reached over to turn on his bedside lamp, but hesitated for a check. He rolled to his right to look at the large pile of Kathy and covers, the elongated lump he jokingly called Mount Kathy. The quilts themselves were so bulky that with only his roll to the right he couldn't be sure whether she was in them. He propped himself up on his right elbow to elevate his head for a better look. There were strands of long dark hair on the slice of the pillow above the quilt.

She was still asleep. He felt a twinge of annoyance at the inconvenience, then a stronger pang of guilt about his self-serving annoyance. Myles would have to get dressed in the dark, always an adventure.

Her arthritis had been worse than usual in the evening. The symptoms would frustratingly drift; last night a new one—she complained about a shortness of breath. Kathy was always cautious about meds, often too cautious, Myles thought. She probably had trouble getting to sleep and was now making up for it. It was important to Myles not to wake her with the noise of his stumbling around in the dark. He smiled at the thought that letting her sleep was worth a few shin bumps as long as he bumped his shins quietly. Myles told people Kathy could hear houseplants grow. The challenge of silence appealed to Myles, a fan of challenges.

Myles would use the scant light of the red clock digits to help him locate the drawers for socks and underwear, his slippers, and the bathrobe hanging on the back of the door. The rest could wait until after coffee. Kathy would be out of bed by then. There was a pivotal moment as he approached the door of the bedroom. It was the moment at which Kathy would wake and turn on her night table lamp, making Myles' silence a wasted effort. He thought the timing of her last-minute waking was too frequent to be coincidental. But for it to be intentional would not be Kathy.

He slowly opened the door, looked back at the lack of motion in the bed, and closed the bedroom door, gritting his teeth at the traditional squeak of the door's hinge. He stood for a moment waiting to hear "I'm up." But nothing. He walked down the stairs to the first floor, started the coffee, and went to his office to get his notes on the day's presentation. He would practice the planned remarks while drinking his coffee.

When Kathy came down, he would go through it again aloud, not looking at his notes, testing his memory. He valued her opinion but was also looking forward to showing her how clever he was with his proposed strategy. She was always complimentary, but might suggest a small change or two, changes he would consider. The suggested changes were never foolish. Once, in a reunion with an old friend, that was his response to the friend's question about her: "She is never foolish."

Kathy the sounding board had helped him retain his sanity or at least lower his pulse rate when he returned from a browbeating by Sanzenbacher. Kathy's sympathy, but more, her serenity, her talent for putting things in perspective, helped Myles to calm down and see that he had, yet again, overreacted.

It was 7:20 a.m. Myles had finished his every-morning two pieces of whole wheat toast. He was surprised that Kathy hadn't come down yet, but was glad that she was catching up on sleep. He would manage to finish his morning preparation silently. He shaved with the spare razor he kept in the downstairs bathroom, then tiptoed up the stairs. A tiny bit of luck, the suit for the day had come back from the cleaners the day before, so he could identify it by the feeling of the cleaner's plastic wrapping. The row of shirts were all white; he couldn't go wrong, so he took one at random, along with a sheaf of ties. One would surely be appropriate. He took it all downstairs and dressed in his office, thinking about the presentation, smiling at his closing line "express ticket to failure;" smiling at the reaction he anticipated.

He would take Kathy out for dinner, something she loved. He could tell her about it and she could share in his triumph. It was not too unrealistic to think that his presentation would lead to a promotion. He would be taking Kathy out to dinner more often.

He had only a few minutes left before he would have to drive to the station. Just time to go back to the bedroom, again silently. If she was still asleep he would very gently kiss her. He felt somehow it would work its way through her sleeping; she would know of it. The bedroom was still dark, too early for light to seep around the shades, and the hair on the pillow had not shifted. He bent over and sensed something was wrong. He very gently shook her; there was no reaction. He turned on her lamp. She looked gray. He put his hand on her chest and could not feel the familiar breathing. He pinched her nostrils to wake her. Nothing. He could not accept it. He threw off her covers, and shouted. He wanted to change what he saw, what had happened, but he could not. It was too late. He knew it, but still stood there, hoping that it was just more of his dream. He knew it was not, but for a few moments could not move. Hope dies slowly.

Myles the planner, the strategist, had not foreseen this. He did not know what to do; he did not know what to feel. He called 911 and had a brief efficient call with the dispatcher. She told him that she would send an ambulance and alert the police.

He was pretty sure that it was too late for an ambulance; she explained that it was a necessary part of the protocol.

He saw that his phone was almost out of charge. Again he had forgotten to charge it, and this made his control slip. He started crying but quickly stopped himself. He plugged in the phone and called his son. He would decide what to say as he waited for his son to answer.

"Junior, it's Dad. Your mother has had a very bad medical emergency. I'll be going to the hospital with her. I'll call again as soon as I know more. I'm going to call your sister now."

"Dad, Kayla is traveling. She's with her college group, helping to renovate houses for the homeless. It won't be easy to reach her. I've got contact info for some of her friends. If it's okay with you, I'll get a message to her."

"Thanks Junior. Please ask her to call me. She's kind of annoyed with me, so it's important that I deliver the message myself."

"Sure Dad. She's not mad at you, just frustrated that you don't accept her values. Give her time. How are *you* doing?"

"I don't know. Numb, I guess."

Myles stood still trying to think of what else needed to be done. He remembered the meeting of the Executive Committee. He thought it would be wrong to tell them that Kathy had died, but "she's in the hospital" might be seen as a lack of commitment to his job.

He spoke to his secretary's voice mail.

"Susie, this is Myles. We've had a family emergency; I won't be able to make it to the meeting."

He heard sirens, sat and waited for the rest of his life to start.

THROUGH AFRICA WITH LUCK AND CREDIT CARD

This is a travelogue, a memoir, originally written for a specific reason and two specific readers, Kip Thorne and Carolee Winstein. They planned to join my wife and me in a jaunt around South Africa eleven years after the end of apartheid. The escapade would follow an international physics conference in the coastal city Durban. Kip had done the travel agent duties which, we soon learned, were yet another of his skills. Unfortunately, a last-minute family emergency kept Kip and Carolee from sharing the adventure directly. With this narration, I hoped to give them some flavor of what they missed. Everything in the memoir is true and accurate, described in a way I hope the reader finds amusing. All places and people are real.

The International meeting GR (General Relativity) 16 was held July 15—21, 2001 in, the ICC, the International Convention Center, in downtown Durban. Six weeks later, eleven years after the end of apartheid, the new center would be the site of the "World Conference Against Racism, Racial Discrimination, Xenophobia and Related Intolerance." The forthcoming conference was getting quite a bit of media coverage due to controversial stances by some participants on Zionism and financial reparation for slavery. By comparison, GR sixteen was little-noted and rather sedate. There were, to be sure, differences of opinions on cosmology, numerical relativity, and the role of string theory, but the outbreak of violence was never at the front of our thoughts. In fact, it was a rather pleasant conference, due in part to the relatively small participation in comparison with other recent GR meetings, and to the togetherness this encouraged.

Durban itself was easily distinguishable from paradise. It had a Dallas-like lack of charm and character. True, it had few Texans, but it had the disadvantage that street crime was a consideration. There were rumors of three muggings of conference participants and at least one of the rumors was multiply confirmed. A Japanese scientist, working in the US, had wallet and passport taken, creating a visa/passport mess for him. Also, Nina, a Danish graduate student, was groped in a bizarre street incident. Nina is not the typical gropee, as she is roughly my size, and looks stronger. This did not make me fear becoming the victim of an ugly incident but why take chances? I walked from the conference site to the restaurants on the beach only with large groups of rowdy Argentines, and—our behavior aside—there were no distasteful incidents.

The general feeling in the air in Durban, and most elsewhere we visited in SA, was the glow of the end of apartheid. On the surface (which is all we saw) there was complete racial harmony and social equality. There was no overt evidence of resentment in the Black population for the white population, despite the abuses of the past and the egregiously skewed distribution of wealth. We were politically incorrect enough to discuss the situation with a number of South Africans, who seemed optimistic, and who unanimously felt that the success, if that's what it turns out to be, would not have been possible without Nelson Mandela.

There were a few burrs on the generally smooth surface. Kids on the beach were begging and had been very obviously coached in how to be adorable and inspire pity. The performance was

transparent but was effective enough to reduce Manuela Campanelli almost to tears.

My wife, here called "the Bee," was to have arrived on Thursday
evening, following the SLC-JFK-Jo'burg-Durban route that I had
taken on the previous Sunday, but her flight into JFK was delayed
and she missed the Jo'burg flight. She chose a route that gave her
a day of touring in Paris and finally arrived in Durban at noon,
Friday. A normal person would have been exhausted and irritable,
but she was elated at the free European vacation. Her roundabout
route took her forty-four hours of traveling. This shattered my old
36-hour travel record but I did not pout for long.

While shattering my record she might have missed the world's
longest nonstop. I was told that the fourteen hour forty-five-mi-
nute flight from JFK to Jo'burg is the longest scheduled nonstop
commercial flight. Interestingly, and consistent with this, is the fact
that the return flight, from Jo'burg to JFK, includes a stop at Isla
do Sal, in the Cape Verde Islands, to slake the plane's thirst. A first
guess was that wind patterns fight the return. I got the right expla-
nation from my seatmate (a federal judge on his fifteenth trip to
do volunteer work helping with judicial infrastructure in Namibia).
According to him, a jet uses a large fraction, 20 percent, of its fuel
just in takeoff. (Can this be?) Since Jo'burg is at some altitude, and
hence has thinner air, it takes more fuel to get airborne, enough to
make a nonstop flight to JFK unwise.

On Saturday, July 21, we took a taxi the few blocks from the
ICC/Hilton conference site to the Avis agency across from the
Royal Hotel, and picked up the car Kip had reserved. As is so often
the case in car rental, it wasn't quite what was expected. Kip had
arranged for a Toyota Venture, and we were given a Toyota Condor. The Venture, we eventually learned, is a very rugged old-style
4WD vehicle. Since we only got stuck in mud once, and not for

long, the 4WD wasn't really needed and the Condor—a very basic, very old-fashioned rear-drive manual-choke power-nothing minivan—was probably the more appropriate vehicle. The throttle on the Condor stuck when the accelerator was pressed too far down, overrevving the engine and adding another constraint to the already over-constrained driving. It was gloriously like the old days. A driver felt needed and it added to the spirit of adventure.

This was my first time driving on the left-hand side of the road, but within a few hours I was doing it correctly more than half of the time, and the sounds of screaming (from the Bee) and screeching (from around us) subsided. The little details (especially the signal stalk on the right hand side of the steering column) were harder than the fundamental issue of left-hand-side of road.

There were things to learn about driving in SA that were related to life and death more than to left and right. SA drivers pass on two-lane (one in each direction) roads, even when there is oncoming traffic. Traffic on both sides just kind of squeezes out on the shoulders to create an extra lane in the middle when someone is passing. The way it is done is much more an exercise in cooperation than in aggression. From their road manners one gets the impression of a fearless, but pleasantly cooperative people, an impression that is confirmed in many other ways.

Saturday, the first day of Kip's African Tour took us up the N2 highway to the Hilltop Camp at Hluhluwe game park. Happily, SA roads are very well marked, and after the first hour or so we had figured out the few idiosyncrasies of road signs, lane markers, etc. The turnoff for Hluhluwe was clearly indicated, and a relatively short drive took us to Memorial Gate, the entrance to Hluhluwe. The road was notable for potholes extending downward to the earth's mantle. The ride back on that road was later to prove more interesting.

As we were driving up the hill to aptly named Hilltop, a real honest-to-God lion loped across the road right in front of us. My reaction was an interesting comment on sociology. I pulled over so that I could get out to look at the lion. Due to the Disnification of America, I had not internalized that this animal was real and could be dangerous. I think this disconnection from reality is linked to the density of lawyers in the US. We believe that we are protected, or damn well should be, from the consequences of any stupid action. Screaming from the passenger seat brought me to my senses before I opened the car door.

We later learned that, as a rough approximation, there are no lions in Hluhluwe. We had anomalous luck probably because a single lioness atypically had just had cubs close to Hilltop and was hanging around.

Our second sighting was even more noteworthy. As we unloaded luggage we chatted with a young SA couple. (It is interesting that the woman was working on improvising a patch for their truck turbocharger, while the man stood alongside, helpless.) They told us that there was a rugby game about to start in the staff area. We should come watch. They pointed to a road and told us to ignore the signs that said "staff only." Excited by an invitation to break a rule, off we went. The road we shouldn't have been on became a dirt road through dense trees. It was getting dark, when I stopped. On the road, a short distance in front of us was the tail end of a huge African elephant. If you are not elephant-aware you may not know that an African elephant is to one of those cuddly Indian elephants the way a bobcat is to a kitten.

Without moving my lips or breathing I said to the Bee in 6-point font: "There's an elephant." She looked up and made a statement I was to mockingly repeat several times in the next few days: "Where's the elephant?" It was so big that she didn't see it. She mistook it for background. It looked like darkness. I saved my mirth for later as we checked out just how fast a Toyota Condor could go in reverse.

Thus, within a half hour of arriving we had seen 40 percent of "the Big Five" (lion, elephant, buffalo, rhino, leopard). Our next sighting was of quantum gravity friend Abhay Ashtekhar and a herd of Indian physicists. This was in the Hilltop dining room. As they were not part of the Big Five, our interest in them was limited.

The terrain around the game park is rolling hills, with quite a few medium-size trees. It must be very green in summer since it retained a dusky green even in the dead of southern winter. The land and landscape were very different from the flat brown grasslands we were later to see in Kruger. This, we were told, is why there are no lions (except for our leonine jaywalker) at Hluhluwe: Lions, and who can blame them, like to run for a while to catch their prey, and the terrain at Hluhluwe was unsuitable. I had much to learn about megafauna.

Before embarrassing ourselves too badly we inferred from what people were saying that the name of the park is pronounced "Shluh-Shlooey," not "Huh-loo-huh-loo-weh." This explained why we had had such bad luck asking for directions. The spelling, by the way, follows the rule for transcribing Zulu words into Latin letters: the letter combination "hluhluwe" is always pronounced shluh-shlooey.

Hilltop Camp itself was a collection of sort-of two-family cabins, tastefully hidden in the woods near the central reception/dining room building. The food at Hilltop, like everywhere in SA was tasty, very inexpensive, and over-plentiful. A good meal, with wine, at a good restaurant was typically less than $15 for two, something like a factor of four less than what it would cost in the US.

At Hilltop, the arrangement is that you sign up for—and pay

separately for—driving or walking tours. Some of the tours were already full, but we signed up for everything we could. This amounted to a day drive, a night drive, and a morning hike. Our driving guide told us his name was Welcome. "Welcome?" we asked. "Welcome," he answered. Or, he told us, we could call him by his Zulu name, Mbhlwhuwemhlmb. We called him Welcome. He was the first of several SA blacks we met whose adopted names were nouns that we didn't think of as people names. We were later to meet "Department" and the unforgettable "Difference." Of course, there were also Phillip, Eric, and Tim.

On the drives, Welcome would point to an infinitesimal dot in the infinite distance and with our 20x50 binoculars we would confirm that there was indeed an elephant or a rhino. Without Welcome, after the first half hour, we would have reported the park devoid of all life. Later, we found big game quite close to the road. Or it seemed close at that time. We were to have our idea of "close" altered at Kruger soon after.

The hike was more interesting than the drives, and we walked within about 10 meters of a giraffe (not scary) and 25 meters of a bull elephant. In an interesting example of non-Euclidean geometry, 25 meters from an elephant is a much smaller distance than 10 meters from a giraffe. When the bull turned, squinted at us, and flared his ears, showing an attitude that was familiar from my youth on the streets of New York City, the 25 meters became microscopic. The guide at that point asked that we back away. The Bee and I were anxious to please.

Hluhluwe forms a sort of dual park with Umfalozi which, disappointingly, is pronounced pretty much the way it is spelled. The two parks, but especially Umfalozi, are the bright spots in the program to rebuild the rhino population and have been successful to the point that the parks have as many rhinos as the land will support. An interesting wildlife sidelight is that elephants were not indigenous to the area, at least not recently, and were introduced to the park. The young bull elephants took to killing the rhinos by stomping them and goring them with their tusks. (Rhinos run faster, but the elephants would ambush the rhinos at mud wallows.) One theory was that the elephants wanting clean water were irked that rhinos messed up the water holes with their wallowing. It was much more likely, though, that the killing was just a manifestation of elephant aggressiveness. Babar is a lie. Elephants are mean.

To deal with the problem, the park rangers introduced old bulls to the park, and these old bulls controlled the young males, stopping the rhinocide. As an old bull, I found this a source of inspiration.

In the middle of our second day—between tours—we drove from the Hluhuwe to the Umfalozi side to see the slightly different sights. Both the Bee and I became confused at the border between Hluhluwe and Umfalozi. There is, in fact, no discontinuity between the parks, but at the point of transition there is the Nyalazi gate with Hluhluwe-Umfalozi on one side and the outside world on the other. It is an alternative to the Memorial Gate further to the northeast. Mistaking this for a gate between the parks we inadvertently exited Hluhluwe-Umfalozi. (In a continuation of this confusion we were to go through that gate a large number of times. After the first few passages, the guard at the gate stopped questioning us and with a resigned expression simply opened the gate each time he saw us approach.)

An advantage of our wrong turns was that we got to see the nature of the Zulu life outside the park. Nothing impressed us quite so much as the 100 km/hr speed limit sign on the dirt road outside the park. These people must have been very fierce warriors.

Here is where we gave our first "jump" (lift) to a hitchhiker. We were to do this several times during our travels and never felt that we were taking any foolish chances, though locals advised us otherwise.

After an even number of passages through the gate, we found our way, inside Umfalozi, to the rhino breeding "bomas." (The word means something like enclosure.) Both white and black rhinos are bred here and are shipped to zoos and game parks. The Bee found the baby rhinos irresistible and they were going for a very reasonable $10,000. I was ultimately successful in convincing her that a rhino would not be happy in Salt Lake City. We were given a tour of the bomas by Bheki, a young guide who told us that we were his first Americans ever. That pleased us but made us hope that Bheki would never get into a conversation about us with the guard at the Nyalazi gate.

Midmorning on Monday, after a morning game drive, we hitched up the Condor and aimed east, on the road that had brought us to the park. There was a new experience on pothole alley. A bunch of preadolescent Zulu kids were dancing and jumping on the road, blocking traffic. (At that moment, we were the only traffic.) They wanted money, but the Bee gave them some drawing materials she had brought as gifts. When we spoke firmly to them they moved out of the way and let us pass.

Our Monday destination was Sodwana Bay Lodge in the Greater St. Lucia Wetlands park. This meant driving back toward the N2 and continuing through the town of Hluhluwe, just east of the N2, out to the Indian Ocean. The guide books warned of 90 km of dirt road, but an excellent road was under construction and only 10 km of dirt road remained.

The weather had turned cold and drizzly, and we seemed to be driving the 10 km of dirt just as school was letting out. There were

Zulu kids in school uniforms (white shirts, dark blue trousers or skirts, sometimes shoes) walking along the road. The rain was getting worse and a group of them made the praying gesture that is used in SA to say "please, please, give me a lift/jump." The Condor became a bus as we squeezed in around six of them, along with a woman who may have been a teacher. The kids spoke some English, and it was one of our moments of insight to see how proud and happy these kids were.

We dropped them off at the town of Sodwana Bay and entered the gated enclosure for the Sodwana Bay Lodge. The "Lodge" was not a building, but rather a collection of around forty rustic thatched huts that seemed to be managed under some sort of condominium or timeshare arrangement. There was a dining room and scuba/diving shop. Deep sea fishing and horseback riding facilities were advertised on billboards just outside.

The weather was continuing to grow worse, but we made plans to go diving the next day. I was going to take scuba lessons, leading to a dive in the ocean, and the Bee, claiming expertise, was going to go out on a dive. The weather continued growing worse. The rain and the temperature continued falling and the winds became fierce. Although the temperature was probably around 40 F, the damp and the winds made us feel flash frozen. We were later told that this was the coldest it had been in Sodwana Bay in ten years. The Lodge facilities were not designed for this. The huts were not even completely closed (the walls did not reach completely up to the thatched roof) and there was no source of heat. The dining room was like the huts. The waitresses wore winter coats and we warmed our hands over a candle on the table. It turned out that on the first night we were the only guests there.

We had brought a reasonable assortment of clothing, but we were encountering unreasonable weather. We did what we could, putting on multiple layers of clothing and looking like two Michelin men. One of my clearest visual memories from the trip is the Bee in a cocoon of clothes, sitting (to the extent she could bend) by an electrical outlet. From the cocoon came the hum of the hair dryer and a moan of thermal ecstasy.

Tuesday dawned but not by much. The winds had not abated and the sea was far too rough for diving. No boats would be going out. The only activity available was horseback riding, so we drove to the small town, really a gas station and a grocery, and signed up for a two-hour nature ride. We ended up going out with 40ish Johnny and 25ish Anne Marie, who kept a small herd of horses within the Sodwana Bay Lodge enclosure, and were training some of the local Zulus in caring for and riding horses. Although it was not part of their background, it turned out that the Zulus loved to ride horses, maybe to the point that it distracted them from the other parts of the job.

It was pleasant. The Bee enjoyed being on a horse, but for me the most interesting part was talking to Johnny about SA attitudes and race relations. It was beginning to dawn on me that sociology in SA was much more complicated than Black vs. White, but included many threads of White vs. White, Black vs. Black, and many shades of gray.

Our bad luck with the weather prevented us from having the experiences we anticipated at Sodwana Bay. On the bright side, malaria was a complete nonissue. Not only were there no mosquitoes but there was no insect life whatever. Polar bears might have been more of a threat.

In any case, the people in the Lodge said that even in warm weather the local mosquitoes were not much of a problem. (This is the opposite of the attitude we heard at Kruger, where malaria, with or without Lariam, is considered an inescapable cost of doing business; you work there, you get malaria. Next question.)

On Wednesday we set off very early partly because the Condor had a heater, but more because the route was a bit daunting. We wanted to avoid being lost after dark, and dark would be coming very early. After taking the 90 km not-much-dirt-left-road back to the town of Hluhluwe we were to follow the N2 to Piet Retief (pyet reTEEF), then to secondary road R33 through Amsterdam to the N17 around Warburton. Next, east on the N17 to the vicinity of Lochiel, then northeast on R541/R38 to Badplaas, then to Barbeton turning north on R40 which we were to follow through Nelspruit to Keipersol, then Hazyview. I estimated an if-no-wrong-turns distance of 600 kms, and estimated our chance of no wrong turns at 3 percent. In fact, we got negligibly lost until within elephant charge distance of our final destination, the Chestnut Country Lodge. One of us (no names, but a short person) expressed concern about taking secondary roads, but the condition of the road and the thickness of the line on the map were not correlated. The "national highway" N2 became rather ragged around Swaziland, whereas R33, R38, etc. were fine roads. (I had been assured of this by Johnny of the horseback riding, who had often made the trip.)

Once near the Chestnut Country Lodge we relied on the Bee's unique "navigation" technique, her "there must be a God" method. In a confident voice, as if she were taking us on a clever shortcut, she barked orders at me to make a set of totally random turns. This continued until we both realized that we were hopelessly lost, though it was forbidden (no names, but the forbidder was a short person) actually to say it. We then stopped and stared at the map for a while. When we thought we had the feeling for the pattern of roads, we looked around for landmarks and found that we were looking at a sign that said "Welcome to the Chestnut

Country Lodge." Variations of this technique were to serve us well again several times.

The trip that appeared so daunting was uneventful. We gave "jumps" to two hitchhikers along the way: a man from the Sodwana Bay highway who was going to the town of Hluhluwe and a woman, with a child, on the road south of Swaziland, who was going a few miles to market. We learned there are informal taxis—minibuses—that prowl these roads and pick up hitchhikers for a small fee.

The woman we picked up tried to pay us. She couldn't speak English and our only Zulu word was Hluhluwe. (Our Zulu vocabulary was eventually to grow to five words, but that was much later.) That word seemed to confuse her, but we eventually worked things out nonverbally.

The road to Hazyview led through the town of Neilspruit, which was a dramatic change from the poor-but-happy villages we had been passing as we drove south of Swaziland. Nelspruit had the architectural feel of Southern California, pinkish and stuccoish, but in a setting much more lush and green. The German luxury car density was high, and there were what appeared to be very wealthy estates/homes. The juxtaposition of wealth and poverty seemed strange until I remembered Manhattan is not so different.

With an hour of daylight left, our tired travelers settled into the luxury of the Chestnut Country Lodge. Our host, Neil (no relation to Neilspruit) of the vedy British affect, was Nth generation South African, and filled us in on white vs. white tension of the old SA. Until thirty years ago, he told us, Afrikaner-background whites and British-background whites were at each other's throats.

Neil, in fact, had been taunted and beaten, every day after school, simply because he had a Dutch-sounding last name. The universal truth would seem to be that schoolboys need to beat up on someone different, and if necessary will make do with a very minor difference.

The setting, the Sabi/e valley (spelled equally frequently with and without the "e"), was romantic enough to inspire Neil to expand his business. Under construction was a "boma" so that weddings could be performed right outside the Lodge, overlooking the valley. Remembering the rhino breeding bomas at Umfalozi, I wondered whether South African weddings might be a bit earthier than our ceremonies, but Neil explained that "boma" means many different things.

Neil's schoolboy poundings had not prevented him from becoming quite a charming person. And quite aside from the beauty of the setting, conversations with him, and with the guests at the Lodge, contributed to the diversity of the Kip African Tour.

The major passion in Neil's life (aside perhaps from his new young wife) was the allegedly famous local double marathon that he had run for something like 20 years. You get a silver medal if you run the marathon in under, let's say, eight hours. (The exact numbers must have fallen out of my head during later travel.) Neil had twelve silver medals. A story from his latest jog seems to me to be metaphoric of the South African spirit. With "only" 10 km or so to go, he came upon a young couple having a spat. She had "hit the wall," become despondent, had taken off her running shoes and thrown them into the woods. Her boyfriend yelled at her, then went on his way to the finish. Neil stopped, helped her search for and find her shoes, and convinced her that she could finish the race, which she went on to do. Prominently displayed on the wall by the bar was a large, beautifully framed, photo of Neil finishing the race, a gift from the lost-shoe young lady. (It seems that the gift rather annoyed the boyfriend, but that might have been the idea.)

A Neil story of another young couple, on honeymoon in a private game reserve, helped prepare us for the Kruger experience to come. On the first day out, hiking with a guide, the newlyweds encountered a rhino who turned and started to charge. The guide yelled for the hikers to scatter and climb trees. The new groom got to one of the few appropriate trees a few seconds after the new bride, who had managed to climb only a short distance. He grabbed her belt, pulled her off the tree and climbed it himself. Though the couple had another week left to their scheduled stay, they left the next day. The epilogue is best left unknown.

Another story involved a group, American women, in which the Bee is reconsidering membership. A few years ago, two post-middle-aged women from New York, and a daughter of one of them, decided to "do" Africa. The women rented a Toyota Camry and drove into Kruger. They were unaware of, or uninterested in, the reality of the terrain and unhesitatingly drove the Camry off road and down a riverbank, where it was parked, in a sense, when the rangers found them. They were standing by a tree pointing to something in the branches, and told the rangers look, antelopes can climb trees. They hadn't noticed, looming over them, the leopard that had dragged the antelope up the tree. I know women like this, and I think that the leopard was frightened.

At and after dinner we formed an alcoholic instant bond with the other guests. When the Bee later asked what the names were of the drunk couple, I told her Richard and the Bee. One of the other two couples was visiting from the UK. The remaining couple, John and Elizabeth, had left the UK twenty-seven years earlier and had lived in various parts of Africa, most recently in Johannesburg, opening the door for questions about crime. John described being robbed at gunpoint at the gate of his home, and made light comedy of it. But then John's work took him to places like the

Congo, where life expectancy (at least for political leaders) is measured with stopwatches. People can get used to lots of different levels of lots of different things.

Thursday morning's activity was ballooning; this had to be done early in the morning when the atmosphere was stable. Contrary to our expectations the balloon ride had nothing to do with viewing big game. We drifted only over the Sabi/e river valley and saw spectacular scenery but no animals larger than a pet dog. I had gone up in a hot air balloon several years earlier at Park City, and this experience was similar: serene rather than exciting. As I was the only one, save our balloon driver, who had been up in a balloon before, I tried to make it more interesting for the other riders by telling them that my friends Kip and Carolee had been killed in a ballooning accident.

The farms (one surprising crop: macadamia nuts) were so beautiful and lush that we mistakenly thought that there was much wealth here, but our balloon captain told us that the farms were too small. Without the economies of scale, the farmers were only just squeezing by.

Our balloon driver was South African middleweight balloon champion, or something, though I never got clear just what one did in such competition. I hope it involved jousting. Whatever it was, he had not done it well when he entered the biggest international competition of his life, in Wisconsin. The exotic setting had thrown him off I suppose. He was a somewhat short, somewhat chubby fellow with a fringe-of-the-face beard. If he had been smoking a clay pipe he could have been a model for a St. Patrick's Day decoration. What with him taking us up in the sky, the Bee couldn't get it out of her head that he was a leprechaun.

I told him that I was a physicist and asked if he had had any interesting experiences with St. Elmo's fire, or ball lightning. He said no to both but described a very different sort of electrical phenomenon. In conditions when the air is very calm, he told me, a balloon crossing over electrical power lines will be deflected to a direction parallel to the lines. This would seem to be an example of dielectrophoresis, the tendency of dielectrics (or for that matter, conductors) to want to move toward a region of higher field strength. I did a rough calculation and found that it was just barely possible. If the lines are very high voltage (hundreds of kilovolts) then the dielectrophoretic force might be as high as a couple of pounds. Maybe this is enough lateral force to push a balloon noticeably in very quiet air.

When the balloon was packed away, we returned to the Chestnut Country Lodge to greet, but softly, our not fully recovered drinking partners of the previous night, and to have a hearty breakfast for the beginning of the heart of our African adventure. The warm-up, the prologue, was now over. We faced the main event.

On Thursday, July 26, a short drive from Hazyview up the R40 took us to Hoedspruit and to the turnoff for Eastgate airport, as in "east gate to Kruger Park." A double fence topped by rolls of barbed wire and a guard tower sent a signal that Eastgate was not your average airport. It is a private airport, but with some strange additional military role we never understood. Its dual purpose probably explained its inconsistencies. The waiting room/ticket counter area was pure mom-and-pop airport, suitable for a once-daily flight of a biplane by a leather-hatted pilot. But the landing strip was large, large enough we were told, for the US Shuttle to land (should the pilot have a sense of direction like mine, I suppose). And the nearby jets were full-size.

We turned in the Condor that had served us so well to a helpful and efficient Avis employee. I was a bit nervous about the unusual airport, but there were no snags. It was an excellent idea to turn in the car. For one thing, even with the Bee's special gift, we may never have found Honeyguide in the maze of identical-looking dirt roads.

We were told that the dirt roads had been fine before the Mozambique floods the previous year. We soon inferred that the locals thought that everyone knew all about the Mozambique floods. I, in fact, had thought that Mozambique was a small island; the Bee thought it was a sports car. We wanted to fit in, so we made sympathetic shakes of the head and muttered something like "Terrible, terrible floods. Yeah. Mozambique." They must been terrible, because the roads now probably cost the transportation company a set of shocks for every Honeyguide delivery. But aside from a few lost dental fillings and short-term double vision, we arrived intact around 2:30 p.m. at Honeyguide Camp. Just in time for lunch.

Honeyguide is not in Kruger Park itself, but in the Minyaleti game park. During the apartheid era, Minyaleti had been the Kruger for the Black population and had been separated from the official Kruger by a fence. That fence was now gone, so the distinction between Kruger and Minyaleti is only a line on a map. The terrain (and hence the fauna) are the same in Minyaleti and in Kruger proper: flat grasslands with scrub brush, small trees, with a few small river beds that are dry in July. It is the prototypical African bushveld, and prime lion country. As we were driven along R531, on our way to Honeyguide, we saw a big ngala madoda (what you would call a male lion) lazily sunning itself on a dirt road visible from the highway.

The camp itself consisted of a central area with a few acres of lawn and a small wading pool. On one side of this lawn is a set of attached medium-size thatched roof structures that serve as the area for meeting, drinking and dining. Across the lawn are a few of the tents for guests. Other tents are off a dirt path that starts from the meeting/dining structure and wends away from the lawn, back into the bush. Our tent was the farthest, something like 100 meters from the central area.

The rule is that you are allowed to walk between your tent and the central area when it is light. But when it is dark you must be accompanied by a rifle-carrying guide; stumbling into wildlife is not encouraged. All guests are told the story of Mrs. Strauss. At a camp like Honeyguide, Mrs. Strauss had been a German tourist who heard the call of (her own) nature during after-dinner brandy. Seeking the ladies room, she ignored the rules. She set out through the dark on her own and was unfortunate enough to stumble into a pride of lions and to disagree with something that ate her. Her husband eventually noticed she was missing and the guides went out with rifles and flashlights to find what was left of her. Strangely, or perhaps not, the event was a great boon to local tourism. Bookings at Kruger area camps shot up and demand was greatest for the camp at which she had been a guest. High premiums were asked for reservations in Mrs. Strauss's cabin.

At the first lunch we met the only other Honeyguide guests at that moment. Fiftyish Mark from Australia was to be leaving early the next day. Not leaving so quickly were British madoda Nigel and mfazi Mary, with daughters Anna and Victoria who appeared to be twins separated by a year. They all had that Queen Mother British accent that makes you think they're really working at impressing you and when they're by themselves they sound as if they're from New Jersey. The girls, Anna and Victoria (aside from having names that sound as if they had been paid for) were into fox hunting. I'm not making this up. Sweet little Anna, braces glinting in the late afternoon African sun, became quite animated when she described the killing of the fox in their last hunt.

But one shouldn't prejudge. Seemingly stuck-up Mary turned out to be funny and a shrewd judge of character. (She communicated with me only by insult.) She and the Bee became best buddies through the shared experience of complaining about husbands, and plans were made to get together in some place like the UK or the US.

After that first lunch we were led along the dirt road to our tent and told that the afternoon game drive would start at 4:00 p.m. Just enough time to powder our noses before boarding the Land Rover back at the central area. True to her philosophy of time (she rounds to the nearest day) the Bee still had a shiny nose at 4:01 p.m., at which point I irritably told her I would see her at the Land Rover, and I took off.

While I'm pretty good about being at the right time, I'm not so good at being in the right place. (On the World Sense of Direction final standings, the only names below mine are daughter Gavi and sister Judy.) At 4:15 p.m., the Bee—muttering "Mrs. Strauss"—sent them out looking for me or for bloody footprints. Sure. It's easy to mock, but don't all dirt roads look pretty much the same? In any case, the Bee stayed quite close for a day or two, until she was certain I knew the way to and from our tent.

One feature of the excellent management of Honeyguide was that the activities were highly structured. (Usually we wouldn't have liked that, but here there was no television set, souvenir shop, or nearby mall.) Days would start with jungle drums (no kidding) just before 6:00 a.m., and we would find tea, coffee and biscuits waiting on the table outside our tent. We would walk through the light-enough dark to the central area and board the Land Rover to start the morning game drive. This lasted from 6:30 a.m. to 9:30 a.m., with a coffee break, in the bush, at around 8:00 a.m. We would return to the central area for a big breakfast from 9:30 a.m.

to 10:30 a.m. and then would indolently loll around until it was 11:00 a.m. and time for our walk with ranger Dave (about whom more later).

On these walks we got much closer to the little stuff, like plants and ticks. On one of the walks we were introduced to the amarula tree that puts out the prototypical tough nut to crack. It seemed to be used in the native culture as a weapon, medicine, money, dice, and more. Of particular interest: It had recently become the basis for a liqueur. The Bee saw in this a way for her to make a solid contribution to local economy. After the walk, at 12:30 p.m. or so, there was time to pick ticks off skin and to shower.

And maybe look at the elephants. Not far from our tent, maybe 80 yards away, there was a small open field, with some water, that served as an elephant hangout. There was a "hide" (what we would call a blind) right at the edge of this field, but why bother with it? We could watch elephant family life while engaged in our own domestic chores in tent sweet tent. It was in this way, while washing socks, that the Bee got to see a mother and baby elephant entwine trunks in something that was apparently so painfully cute that the Bee could describe it only with those high pitched sounds that women use when talking to babies and for greeting acquaintances they haven't seen for several years and don't really like anyway.

After the long lazy afternoon we would gather for lunch from 2:30 p.m. to 3:30 p.m., then assemble for the evening game drive. It went from 4:00 p.m. to 7:30 p.m., with a break roughly in the middle for a "sundowner." This is a South African custom we've really got to import: having a drink while watching the sun go down. Then back to the camp at 7:30 p.m. to sit around the campfire with (surprise!) drinks and then to be served a gourmet dinner. Tired but happy, and very full, our weary campers would be led back to their tent by rifle-toting ranger Dave to rest up for another rough day of being driven around and fed.

The tents themselves were perfect (though they brought back memories to the Bee, whose first comment was "We're at Girl Scout Camp!"). They were canvas tents on cement platforms. A bathroom, enclosed in cement walls, was on the platform but outside, and behind, the tent. The living quarters were rustic enough so that we felt good about ourselves, but they were perfectly comfortable. At night the rule was that the tents were to be zipped closed, front and back, and in the front the zipper tabs had to be fastened to each other with a carabiner-like clip. This was to bar the vervet monkeys who had learned to undo zippers; the clips make the closure monkey-proof. (No doubt some Nobel-prize vervet will soon make the conceptual breakthrough, and the man-monkey battle of wits will escalate.) At the back of the tent a clip was not necessary, and this is interesting. The back of the tent was blocked from external view by the bathroom and the cement wall around it. The vervets, the theory goes, were uncomfortable in a space where they couldn't see what was coming, so they wouldn't hang around the back tent flap playing with the zippers.

The cement platform extended in front of the tent as well as in the back (for the bathroom), and the forward extension made a sort of porch where one could, for instance, watch a mother and baby elephant entwine trunks, or could encounter Albert.

The camp was protected from thieves and poachers by three armed guards. One of them, Albert (I think it was an Anglicization of Albmhlwmhofziwuh) was about six-foot-nineteen, jet black, never spoke or changed his facial expression, wore dark clothes, and carried a rifle that could have stopped a glacier.

Albert was the color of night, so it was quite easy to walk into him on the front porch when one was returning to one's tent after dinner (and sundowners and campfire drinks). In fact, we walked right into him every night, which made us gasp, generate a lot of adrenaline, and think that there was more going on here than met the dark-adapted eye. Why did Albert just happen to be standing on our porch just when we returned, led by ranger Dave, each night? Albert was never there at any other time. (Since he was essentially invisible, we couldn't really be sure he wasn't there without poking around in the dark, or perhaps calling out "Yo, Albert," things we were reluctant to do.) We had our suspicions about how Dave and Albert got their chuckles.

Though no one made up for the departure of Lord Nigel and Lady Mary, there were other interesting guests passing through Honeyguide. Our four-night stay seemed to be a bit longer than typical. Ranger Dave said with disgust that some people would come for a single night and expect to see the Big Five on their first game drive. To amuse him I entered in the guest book "Was here four nights and never saw tigers! Also, at these prices there should be TV." Then I signed the Bee's name.

Guests Lee and Alan were a young couple from Cape Town, she a travel agent checking out the Kruger area camps, and Alan a marketing exec. Young, sleek, Christine and Stoller were from Norway. Toward the end of our stay, beautiful Italian/Cuban Isabel arrived after seeing her husband off in Senegal at the start of the Paris-Dakar rally. We're really talking jet set here. The Bee and I would walk the walk back to the tent attempting a Richard Pryor accent as we amused the loitering buffalo with "Cool? Yeah, we cool!" Our American exclusivity was compromised briefly by the quick passage of Mark, Idaho's wildlife veterinarian, through Honeyguide on his way to "trail camp," one of the alternatives to Honeyguide in Minyaleti.

Honeyguide is the best run and most comfortable of the choices, a judgment that was confirmed by a minor international incident. A strange group of sort of Romanians arrived. (As they were not in our clique—the young and the beautiful—we never found out all the details.) In this group was the Romanian minister of health and his Japanese wife. They had been booked into one of the other camps and had thrown a fit (no tigers, no TV), so their guides/keepers had moved them into Honeyguide for a day. Fine, they said in Japanese-accented Romanian. But the problem was that more guests were to arrive the next day at Honeyguide; there was no room for these camp hoppers. The hell you say, they said, and they refused to leave. Then Bert, the Honeyguide owner/manager/philosopher had to threaten to bring in the police, who all looked like Albert. The rowdy Romanians retreated.

Bert was a typical South African, in that his was not the simple narrow one-track life we expect in people. Bert, the former big game guide, also had a long career as a flight attendant. This sounds comically irrelevant as preparation for his present career, but may not be. Honeyguide was so great largely because management (a/k/a Bert) understood that the product he was selling was a good time. Maybe the flight attendant experience with personal service is what later served him so well.

The heart of the Honeyguide stay, and hence of our African experience, was the game drives. These were in the hands of ranger Dave and trackers Eric or Phillip, and on the 8-ply treads of Bertha, our Land Rover Defender 110. Bertha was made of steel the thickness of lasagna and had tree-climbing real 4WD, not that of the mobile telephone booths of suburban soccer moms. The flat grasslands and scrub vegetation were all pronounced "road" by Bertha, so ranger/driver Dave was unconstrained in his attempts to take us close to nature.

Phillip, ranger Dave's usual faithful smiling Zulu sidekick, was away for our first three days and was replaced by Eric. Eric's mild manner, slight build, slight stoop, and wire-rim glasses were an excellent antidote to stereotyping. On a multiple-choice test, you would complete "Eric is…" with "an accountant" regardless of the other choices. Phillip, of the road smile, was a bit more outgoing, but still far from what central casting would have come up with to fill the role "Zulu tracker."

The tracker sat in a special seat, suspended in front of Bertha's left front fender. This made him an hors d'oeuvre for lions, but the seat gave him a better view of the ground, so that he could look down at the random pattern of bumps in the dirt and announce "two rhinos passed here four days ago; one was thinking of giraffes," or whatever. Ranger Dave showed us some basics of reading the trail and how to distinguish the tracks of, say, female lions from, say, rocks. Toward the end of our stay, I got the hang of this and was able to identify the track of a North American Bee by the characteristic tread pattern of her hiking boots, especially if I had just watched her lift a boot from the pattern. I demonstrated this for tracker Phillip. Still holding the Bee's leg as proof, I pronounced the track to be that of a heavy elderly mfazi. Phillip said something in Zulu that I didn't want translated. The Bee said something in English.

The key people in the game drives were the guides Dave and Chris. Dave was from the British side of the white population and Chris from the Afrikaner side. They were both fluent in both languages, though Chris had a very very slight accent in English. (For all we knew Dave had a very very slight accent in Afrikaans.) When business got particularly heavy (due, for instance, to Romanians) Bert himself did a guide stint.

Our guide Dave, aside from Bert, was the one most responsible for the stay. He was anxious for us to have a good time, and in the Bee's case this meant seeing lots of birds. No problem; it turned out that Dave was also a birder. We would be on a game drive hoping to see the bloody drama of life and death played out by mega-ton beasts when Dave would stop the Land Rover to point out to the Bee something like the 1/2 oz Worthingham's right winged flophopper, much to the, let's call it, amusement of the other guests who were chanting "Li-on, Li-on…"

Dave, and Afrikaans-leaning Chris, were interesting wildlife in their own right. They seemed to be in their mid-20s (as does everyone under fifty nowadays) and were a mixture of kid and professional, not quite sure of their position on the food chain. The wildlife guide business is still developing infrastructure, so that certification as a guide was available but not required. Dave was certified and tut tutted much about his irresponsible colleagues who weren't. This certification meant that David could and did point out to his grateful clients the Latin names of every twig. At other times he and Chris would reminisce about four-day hangovers.

Our attitudes evolved through our succession of game drives. On the first drive we got all excited upon seeing the most common antelope, the mpala. (The western name "impala" is remarkably close to the Zulu name, adding evidence, to my way of thinking, that the continents were once joined.) By the last game drive we kind of considered mpala to be trash game, not worth a turn of the head. To some extent the same could be said of the jillions of Cape buffalo, except that I never tired of the way they looked: dumber than tree stumps. You could look deeply into their eyes and see their tails.

But the must-see animal, of course, is the lion, and Dave felt frustrated that we didn't see a lion on Thursday night or Friday morning. The camp people know the habits of lions and communicate via radio with each other and with guides from other area camps, so that there is very little mystery left about the lion whereabouts. The Minyaleti lions have so little privacy that the guides know pretty much when the lions are hungry and will have to make a kill. In this way, by Friday night, July 27, we were assured that the lions were ready to party. With some hints from other guides, Dave picked up the male early in our night drive. The lion was walking, steady as you please, along the dirt roads for the same reason that people would: it's easier than walking through the bush. The lion just walked and walked, and we just followed and followed. The lion was illuminated, bright as daylight, in our headlights and spotting beam so that it was like a scene from a reality cop show and we were going to cuff the lion.

Dave thought we had it made at this point, but Leo went across a dry riverbed at one of the few places Bertha couldn't follow. So we had seen a lion in the wild, but we had not seen a pride eating. That was remedied the following morning for Yr Hvmble Srvnt, but not for his smaller companion. Late Friday night the Bee went on an unintentional instant African weight loss program. She spent much of the night in the bathroom behind the tent making strange sounds. At first I thought that she was practicing Zulu, but the sounds were her nonverbal message that I should go on this one game drive without her; she would stay behind and work on losing more weight.

But ah, this one game drive involved brunch with Leo and Laura. The pride was found lunching on a freshly killed waterbuck (a medium-size antelope). We were *this* close. The point here is that the lions were completely habituated to Land Rovers full of people. The lions had accepted that the vehicles were neither prey nor danger, so were irrelevant… as long as no unexpected action took place. At a later roadside kill we were to see the reaction to unexpected behavior. A big Rover from a less professional camp than Honeyguide brought a gaggle of tourists to the kill. These tourists had not been told, or convinced, that the deal with lions is for people to stay seated. Joe Tourist stood up the better to videotape or whatever, and a young male immediately snapped to attention locking his radar on the videotaper. Ranger Dave yelled at him to sit down, and he did, leaving my curiosity hanging about what would have been Act II.

On Saturday morning there was no such faux pas. We sat in (more like on) the open Land Rover, which began to feel like a snack tray. There were lions in the grass around us. The nearest one was maybe 10 feet away, but was focused completely on butt of waterbuck, and paid no attention to us. There were, of course, the little family incidents that characterize the lives of these, the only social cats. A presumptuous advance here, a growl there, as the teenagers checked out the limits, and Leo, Laura, and Aunt Lucy repeated that they could not have the car keys.

Later in that morning's game drive we stopped to look at I forget what. Ranger Dave pointed to a strange kind of fluffy bird and was uncharacteristically failing in his identification prowess until he realized that it was the tip of the tail of a leopard in the tall grass. We followed the leopard for a few minutes and got a great view until it disappeared at a river line.

Two things are important here. First, this is a magnificent animal. It is much more beautiful and frightening than a lion. And much wilder and more unpredictable. You can laugh at a lion; you just gasp at a leopard. Second, the leopard is by far the most difficult to spot of the Big Five (elephant, rhino, buffalo, lion, leopard). The reason this is particularly important is that the Bee's digestive indisposition prevented her from seeing the leopard and therefore from joining the Big Five club. I consoled her with the words nyaaa nyaaa. I saw the Big Five. You didn't. (The Bee later became very tiresome pointing out that she saw a cheetah and a hippo—in separate incidents, I think—and I didn't. Cheetah, hippo, ho hum.)

Waterbuck had been a snack for the lions, so we were assured that the pride was getting ready to rumble again, and soon after that a dead buffalo was found just off the road near the park gate. On Saturday night there were no lions at the carcass, but something was going on. We prowled the park and ran into the pride before dark. It was a variation of our earlier lion-in-the-light experience. Now we were

traveling the road with four lions. Dave pulled over to the side of the narrow dirt road so the lions could walk past. (We would be turning off in another direction.) There is an interesting rush of adrenaline and glow of unreality as you sit completely exposed in (on) a vehicle and lions walk by close enough that you could pet them (in your last few seconds of life).

Ranger Dave reasoned that they were eating something and needed to drink. Since it was the dry season, there were few places for this and in a brilliant extrapolation of the lion trajectories, Dave put us at the likely water hole just as the sun went down. The darkening African sky was brilliant orange, as we sat in/on the Land Rover sipping cocktails and watching a big male lion lapping water in a large version of our kitten drinking. Thank you, Dave.

Sunday morning I awoke with a painful lower back, and took my turn at missing a game drive (the cheetah/hippo game drive, if I am so foolish as to believe the Bee). Sunday night we were after an answer to the question: whither the buffalo carcass. This time was the charm. About half the carcass was already gone, and we watched three lions tear chunks of meat and viscera off what was left. Second only to the exciting incident of the standing videotaper, the scene is memorable for the aroma of Eau de Long Dead Buffalo.

Being out among the lions certainly did move one's heart

monitor up a notch, but terror was (at least for me) limited by the thought that the lion would lose interest before getting to me. After all, tracker Phillip was suspended out in front, and was the equivalent of bait. Should the lion still be looking for trouble, Dave in the driver's seat would have been a natural next step. Killing me, three rows back, and a few feet higher, would have strained the lion's attention span.

Such considerations didn't apply to elephants. You want to be scared? Go find an elephant. The best example was the Head Shake Incident. Early in the evening drive we came upon a large bull and a juvenile bull, in the bush quite close to the road. Dave stopped the Land Rover. It seemed to us that we were foolishly close to this animal that wouldn't need any exceptional effort to kill us all and eat the Land Rover. But Dave seemed perfectly relaxed as he prattled on about elephant behavior. We took some comfort in the fact that Dave, who had never been killed by an elephant, was something of an elephant psychologist. Dave pointed out how relaxed the big bull was as it uprooted trees. In retrospect, this moment of relaxation illustrated a human trait. Honest people assume, as the default, that other people are honest. Crooks assume that other people are out to get them. Laid back Dave, looking into himself, figured that all life forms were relaxed.

But the big bull elephant was faking it. He stomped out of the bush onto the road, right behind the Land Rover to within a tusk length from us, and showed an expression equivalent to "You have a warrant?" Dave chuckled at his own misjudgment. Though the bull wasn't relaxed, Dave was. About this time that it occurred to me that Dave would be perfectly relaxed if lions were ripping him apart.

To help us appreciate what we would see next, Dave told us that the elephant would probably make an aggression display. This time he got it right. The elephant took a step toward us and shook its head rapidly a few times to show that it was boss, and that the boss was mad. The shaking head was slightly closer than we might have liked. We might have liked it to be at the edge of the visible universe. The Bee dealt with this using the technique that she had perfected in her three attempts to sit through the "Blair Witch Project." She put her hands over her eyes and made a sort of humming sound.

It is good that she didn't rest her eyes too long. Comedy was about to follow terror. The tiny (three tons, maybe four) juvenile was serving a sort of apprenticeship to the big bull. This is how they learn to be elephants. (They can't read.) So little Dumbo set out to do just what big Bubba had done. He followed exactly the same path out of the bush and right up to the back of the Land Rover. He then tried to give a head shake but almost fell over. Embarrassed, he retreated to the bush to practice. We did not laugh. Daddy might have thought it rude.

Then there were the native languages. We heard tell primarily of Zulu (most common) and Xhosa (second most common, native language of Nelson Mandela). Also often mentioned was Swati (Swaziland variant of Zulu), and something that sounded like "Sangan." (The books list languages named "San," "Tsonga," and "Sandawe." It could have been any or all.) Statements made to us about language were not always fully consistent. On the relationship of Zulu and Xhosa, for example, we heard two different shades of opinions: (i) They are completely unrelated, and (ii) They are almost identical. According to the web both are part of the Bantu language group, so the latter is probably closer to the truth. (If there is any meaning to truth here.)

In any case, we were in the province of KwaZulu-Natal most of the time, and Zulu was the dominant language. Of course, we picked up a few words. We didn't want to sound like gringo tourists so we tried to get the pronunciation right. This was difficult. It involved Bushman type clicks, clicks that according to always helpful linguists "…may be dental, palatal, alveolar, lateral, labial, or retroflex; voiced, voiceless, or nasal; aspirated or glottal." Back at Honeyguide I practiced these in the tent and swear that I heard the sound of Albert laughing somewhere outside, although it was something I couldn't picture. After some time, I had no trouble with the clicks except for those that were dental, palatal, alveolar, lateral, labial, retroflex, voiced, voiceless, nasal, aspirated or glottal.

We eventually learned the words madoda (male); mfazi (female); schlegimfazi (cackling old female, a word still in use by one of us); ngala (lion); and nQgorno. (I don't know what this last one means, but the "Q" indicates a click and I got to the point that I could say it to my satisfaction, though only to mine.)

A shadow of doubt was cast over the language proficiency we had struggled to attain. Ranger Dave had told us that "ngala" was lion, and we heard the word many times. We really got into it. As lions walked by the car we would mutter in the deepest voice our fear would allow "mmmmm ngala madoda and ngala mfazi." But the dictionaries say that the Zulu word for lion is "ibhubesi" and the Xhosa word is "ingonyama." This raises certain questions. About "vrdoodoo," for instance.

There are three kinds of hornbills in the Kruger area. The Bee gave the impression that her death (something she thought was imminent) could not be happy unless she saw all three. Early in the game drives she saw two of them, something like the golden hornbill and the matriculated hornbill. She yearned for the elusive ground hornbill. Ranger Dave told her that the Zulu word for this bird was "vrdoodoo." Each time the Bee got into (onto?) the Land Rover she would say to Eric or Phillip, in her impeccable Zulu accent, "vrdoodoo." They would respond, sounding something like television Tonto, "mmmmm…vrdoodoo." I suggested to the Bee that vrdoodoo sounded suspicious and that it was similar to the term for "car," used by the rabbits in "Watership Down." She countered that Eric and Phillip appeared to understand the word. But there are many explanations. Late at night I thought I heard sounds of helpless laughter and much slapping of knees from the area where the guides and trackers hung out.

After four days of smoothly roughing it, we were having trouble remembering

life with no elephants in the back yard and no one waiting on us hand and foot. It was Monday, July 30, time to move on to Cape Town, so back to the strangeness of Eastgate airport, and forward snaglessly to Cape Town.

If Kip's purpose in juxtaposing Kruger and Cape Town was contrast, he did well. Not too many comparisons could have beaten this. Maybe North Dakota/New Delhi. The Cape Town area isn't real. It's a Disney theme park based on some of the best parts of the US: northern California, New England, and Iowa. The city is built more or less around Table Mountain, a flat-topped, sheer-walled feature that dominates everything. We hit Cape Town on Tuesday morning in Full Tourist Mode; the gondola up Table Mountain was check mark No.1. But high winds and rushed schedule meant we had to move on to check mark 2. We'd have to return to Cape Town someday.

We drove south along the east side of the peninsula (that of "False Bay" and the Indian Ocean) down to the Cape of Good Hope, or as the Afrikaans signs said: Kaaap uhvf Goeuad Hoeup (spelling approximate, as always in Afrikaans). En route we stopped to see the penguins at Boulders beach. In a way, this was a continuation of an adventure of three years ago. Near the Valdez

Peninsula of Patagonia we had gone to Punto Tombo to see two jillion Magellenic penguins in their night-of-the-living-dead march between sea and nest. We had been up close with the Magellenics, and had developed personal relations with them. One had lovingly nuzzled Betsy, and another had bitten me. The jackass (for their braying sound) penguins of Boulders beach were close cousins by marriage to the Magellenics, and we were around the same latitude, so it was all vaguely like seeing a flip side. If it hadn't been for the Patagonia experience we probably would have had a "Gosh Martha, real penguins!" reaction. But as it was, we forced a superior smile and said, "How nice, a few penguins."

The Kaap was also somewhat a sequel. On our Patagonia peregrination we had gone to Ushuaia, the southernmost city in the world (don't believe the Chileans about Port Williams), had seen Tierra del Fuego, and the Beagle channel. So tips of continents were a specialty, and now we were adding the African tip. And adding it at some risk. The walk from the tourist parking lot to the actual certified, been-there-done-that Cape was about a mile along a high, completely exposed rocky path swept by the same 200 mph winds that had kept us from taking the gondola up Table Mountain. Perhaps they fell short of 200 mph, but they were enough to keep images in our mind of being swept off the rocky path into the sea, a long, long way down, and of cracking our heads open on the dotted line dividing the Atlantic from the Indian Ocean. It would be a hell of a dramatic way to die, but we still had things to see, so we filled our pockets with rocks, didn't look down, and have now added another continent tip. Look out Asia.

The menu for Wednesday, the second day, was whale and wine. The town of Hermanus, at the top of False Bay, was an old whaling village and was a frequent haunt of old Southern Right Whales (Balaena S. Rightus, or something like that). It was as if we were seeing déjà vu again. We had bumped into (just about literally) a S. R. Whale on the Valdez Peninsula. (Actually in the waters of the Golfo Nuevo off the Valdez Peninsula.) In fact, we even knew a S. R. Whale by name. Our Argentine Balaena was called "Tenedor" (Spanish for fork) for a fork-shaped white dorsal marking. Tenedor came right up to our boat and no kidding seemed to like to be around people. There was no "don't get between the momma and her cub" here. Tenedor (Tenedora?) was a new mother back then and we got to see cetacean maternal love; she seemed to be proudly showing off her new whalino to the boat.

Wouldn't it be a blast to run into Tenedor here? Maybe reminisce? Two realities got in the way. First, we were told by the local experts that the shiftless male SRWs do bounce around between continents, but the females stay close (1000 miles) to home. Second, there were no whales to be seen that day anywhere near Hermanus.

Time moved on, and so did we, to the day's second activity: a tour of a vineyard. We drove to Stellenbosch, the center of the wine growing region and we aimed for the well-hidden "wine tour information center." A prohibitionist society must have been responsible for placing this center and for putting up the signs with directions to the center. We drove back and forth on the main street of town from 1:00 p.m. to 2:00 p.m. till we spotted a sign the size of an index card stating "wine tour information." We made the indicated turn and found ourselves in a complicated area with several streets any of which could have hidden many wine information centers with room left for an invading army. We said bad words about Stellenbosch and agreed to head back to Cape Town (though we weren't agreeing on much else at that point). Of course, we immediately found ourselves looking right at the "wine tour information" center not far off. It was a déjà vu of stumbling across the Chestnut Country Lodge. Mystical magic? The Bee's navigational blessing?

It was 2:24 p.m. and the last tour started at 2:30 p.m. We made it on time by relaxing some of the pickier guidelines for driving, such as the recommended side of the road. Many people honked their appreciation.

We greatly enjoyed ourselves making disparaging remarks about the wine ("this would go well with dysentery," "fruity, with a hint of sewage") but our grumpiness faded as our consonants got fuzzier and by the time we headed back to Cape Town most was forgiven the Stellies.

Thursday morning was appropriately gray. It was our last day in Africa. There was much we hadn't seen, and the Bee considered it a sign of failure that we had money left. We saddled up, ran through the castle (the original Dutch East India Company fort), sprinted past the museums, drove around in several circles. And in such insipid touristy activity did we spend our last few hours in Africa. But these hours were not typical. There had been Hluhluwe, there had been Sodwana Bay, there had been Hazyview, and most of all there had been interesting people.

BUSTER

I'm not going to win any prize for saying this, but life's funny. You never know what's going to happen next. Maybe something good. It's a reason to stay around. Know what I mean? Just in case. Let me tell you about my friend Stanley. He's thirty-eight years old and finally last November finds a girlfriend. Seriously, he's thirty-eight and she's his first girlfriend. Helene. So it's damp and cold in Dorchester, but for Stanley the sun is shining, birds are chirping. (Yeah, we got birds.) The sky is blue, but out of the blue Helene ups and leaves him, calls it quits. Lasted just one month.

I guess a friend would've asked him why she left. I maybe forgot to ask, or maybe figured he'd tell me. Don't really remember, but remember this: Talk about prizes. You ask me Helene should win one for staying with Stanley a month.

So, anyway, he's real down—no surprise—and wants to pack it all in. Not real original, but you can't find a duck much stranger than Stanley. He takes books out of the library on how to kill yourself. Goes back a couple of times. Maybe you'd think a librarian would notice and get worried, but they only notice if you raise your voice.

So he's going for a merit badge in suicide and it's distracting him at work. Work is doing data entry at some accounting company for more than minimum wage, but not much more. Part of his job is changing the toner cartridge in the copier. How to is printed on the inside of the cover you open to get to the toner, and there's clear pictures. Also a motherly secretary takes pity and shows him how the first time.

But Stanley's distracted with how he's going to off himself and it doesn't occur not to hang on to the machine when he leans over backwards to lower himself so he can see the stuff inside. The machine falls on him and breaks his leg. On the way to the hospital he sees an ad on a bus. Some lawyer says Injured? Call me. Stanley says the phone number over and over to himself; has it memorized by the time he's at the hospital.

To make a short story short, the judge—the one the call-me lawyer angled for—said it was the fault of the accounting company for not training him. Stanley said the accounting lawyer spent most of the hearing rolling his eyes. Stanley's call-me lawyer asked the eye-roller if anyone told Stanley not to lean over backwards. The guy answered something that insulted Stanley and upset the judge.

Bottom line: Stanley has to spend the rest of his life in a wheelchair when anyone's watching. The judge said the company was negligent. That's what he prob'ly said. I wasn't there, and Stanley couldn't remember for sure.

So Stanley gets a nice check every month for being disabled from an accident on the job and for negligence. Sure, it's no fun being in a wheelchair, but it's more fun than being dead. Just a little before, he was going to kill himself and now Stanley can stay home and do whatever he wants. Pretty funny. Life.

By the way, for a couple of weeks after he was sitting pretty—manner of speaking—he tried calling Helene. Bunch of times. Finally she answered, told him she was sorry for his accident but she had a new boyfriend. Might've been true. Fell right off Stanley's back like water off a strange duck. He asked me to return his books to the library. His attitude had changed. I'll say it again. Life is pretty funny.

Well that's sort of how it was with Buster. Kind of like an accident. Didn't see it coming.

I was feeling kind of down. Not like I was taking those books out of the library—though it would've been fun to see the librarian's face. Just that every week was like every other week. Same. Same. Same. I felt like I was suffocated by same. It was creepy thinking nothing was going to change. I figured maybe part of it was I didn't have lots of friends. In fact, Stanley was the only one, and I didn't see him much anymore. The wheelchair bothered me. Not that he needed it. What bothered me was he didn't.

So I decide to get a cat. This time I'm going to do it right, get a good one, not like the mistake I made at the animal shelter two years ago when I picked up Stinky. But when I get to the pet store I see Buster. I'm not going to lie and say I knew how special he was right off. Wouldn't be completely true, but I did notice him right off.

The pet store has a big window on the street, and they put the puppies in little bins right up against the window. I guess the pet store people think someone will be walking by and say "Hey, I'm gonna get me a puppy," the way they wouldn't need a big plan just to buy a donut. People did look at the puppies, and the puppies looked at the people. Even more.

This next part is going to make me seem stupid, so let me just push it right out there and get it over with. I'm thinking Buster had his face all pushed in from pressing his nose against the window. The pet store owner, a nice woman, tells me Buster is a bulldog puppy and that's the way he's supposed to look.

I'm trying hard to concentrate on cats, but every time I look back to the front of the store I see Buster. He's not looking out of the window anymore. He's looking into the store, and he's staring at me with that cute pushed-in face. I never had a chance.

I'm not good at buying stuff. My mother always said the swindlers could see me coming a mile off. When she was in one of her good moods she'd say it's cause I'm trusting. Usually she wasn't in a good mood and she'd say I'm gullible. I liked that word better than the one she used when she was in one of her really bad moods.

Anyway, I try to be careful not to get taken in, so I play it cool when I ask about pets. I want to kind of keep it to myself I really want that puppy. The lady I talked to seemed real nice, but I guess that's what makes the best swindlers. I pretend the question about Buster was just curiosity, and I'm here to look over cats. Then I waste about a half hour of her time pretending to be interested in cats. You know, asking questions. How much does this one shed? Is that one good with kids? I kind of feel bad about my pretending, and feel even worse cause she was prob'ly seeing I'm phony cause I wasn't good at it. But she liked talking about the cats, so it wasn't so bad.

Finally, I tell the nice lady none of the cats appeals to me though they all seem good (I didn't want to insult her.) Then, cool as I can, I say maybe I should consider another kind of pet. She plays right into my hand when she says how about a puppy. And, still acting not real interested, I say, "Hmmm. A puppy? Like, just for example, how much is that puppy with the pushed-in face?"

She says $800, and I am definitely no longer cool when I repeat the cost very very loud and kind of embarrass her. I apologize of course.

She tells me $800 is a real bargain for a pure bred English bulldog. According to the lady, Buster was marked down from $1200 (I almost shout again) cause English bulldogs were not the hot items right then. Some other kind of dog was drawing all the business cause that kind of dog was on a TV show. So this month everyone's trying to buy that kind, and every other kind is sort of on sale. I check later and find out it's true; $800 is a bargain. And Buster has papers. Up till then I don't know what this means, having papers. Turns out papers list his parents, grandparents, great grandparents and more, maybe back to the dog Adam and Eve kicked around with. What's funny I only know back to my grandparents. Of course, his name isn't Buster on those papers, it's "Rollingbrooke's Captain Stavro." But I call him Buster, and right from the beginning he likes the name. No mistaking it.

There I was. I really wanted Buster, but I was not crazy. I can't spend more on a dog than I spent on my car. The lady sees I'm worried about the money, and she tells me Buster's an investment. I can use him as a stud dog. She explains to me what that means, and I am kind of embarrassed. Anyway, that's how I let myself spend $800 on a dog. He's not a pet; he's an investment.

No surprise, I didn't have $800. I call my sister and tell her about my investment in a stud dog. I have to hold the phone away from my ear cause she's yelling so loud. I could hear words like gullible. At least that's what I hope I heard from the held-out phone. Anyway, she caved in. But it involved a long lecture on responsibility and making wise choices. I can't really remember the details.

Long story short, a few days later I am walking out of that pet store with my new investment and almost $100 in dog odds and ends, and the book *You and Your New Bulldog*.

I never was sorry for a minute that I went into hock to my sister for a bundle. Buster made me so happy. He was a great friend (like the bulldog book said), and I went a little bit overboard in the pride department. When people stopped me on the street to say how cute, I would show them Buster's papers.

That was the simple start but then life turns funny up a notch.

A guy comes to the door, respectable looking guy. He's selling raffle tickets, tells me he's from the police, and he says the profits go to widows and orphans of cops killed on the job. I figure (prob'ly like everyone else) this is a good cause, and if I buy a $10 ticket I get a sticker for my car bumper. I'm no dummy. I figure the sticker might be worth a lot more than $10 if I'm trying to talk my way out of a traffic ticket, maybe cause my car stalls on the highway again.

So, I'm scrounging in my wallet for $10 and Buster begins to threaten. He was kind of growling in the back of his throat soon's I open the door, but now starts in like he's going to rip the guy's heart out. The guy takes off, with me yelling after him I'm sorry. But later, I'm watching TV and there is this news there's a bunch of scammers selling fake raffle tickets and saying they're from the police.

Did Buster know the guy was lying? Was my new best friend an animal lie detector? I had to check this out, so we went to visit Stanley. A couple of years ago, Stanley had borrowed my Dremel tool to put his name on some of his stuff. I take Buster over to meet Stanley and I'm going to ask for my Dremel back. When I do this Stanley tells me he already returned it and I just forgot. He adds details, you know? The way people do when they are good liars. Stanley says stuff like "Don't you remember? You were in a rush when I came over to return it, and you were having trouble with your car." Stanley isn't going out on any limb with the car trouble, and though he's doing a good job of it, I suspect he's lying. Then I look over at Buster. Sure enough, Buster has a scowl. He's not barking like with the raffle guy but I figure he's just too polite to bark at a "friend." And Buster's expression was a real clear scowl. No mistaking it. But Stanley doesn't have a clue, and it was sort of sad. Stanley took a real shine to Buster. You could almost see what was going through Stanley's head: "I should have Buster."

Around this time I get a call from the nice lady at the pet shop. She says there are some people who want to breed their English bulldog "bitch." (I learned this word is okay, but it still embarrasses me.) The pet lady asks if I am interested. I still owe my sister $580, so yeah, I'm interested. The pet store lady sets up a meeting, and she doesn't charge any money for it. Like I said, nice lady. The people who want Buster's help are going to come to visit me to see Buster's papers and everything.

At first, I'm excited about this. Sure the money would be nice, but it's not only the money. I keep thinking Buster's going on a date. Cause, you know, that's sort of what it is, right? Sort of. They're dogs, so it's kind of different, but it's also kind of the same. I remember getting ready for the junior prom in high school. (I didn't go to the senior prom.) I remember getting all dressed up, and how nervous I was, and how I didn't know how to behave and what to do. Didn't have a clue. That was around fifteen years ago, but I still remembered. I had a kind of lousy time. Probably it's not going to be anything like that for Buster, what with him being a dog, but who knows. Anyway, it took some of the edge off me feeling so good about this.

More edge comes off on the weekend. The Highsmiths drop by to talk about Buster and their lady English bulldog. They come on a weekend, cause I have to work on weekdays. He says he works from home. I'm polite, so don't say anything, but if you're at home, you're not at work. Anyway, they seem nice, if great clothes mean nice. They are a married couple. I keep wondering if he married her so they could breed. Shows how much my mind was locked onto this stud breeding thing. Of course, I don't say anything, even accidentally. It's important to be polite.

They keep looking around and saying things like "charming," but I can tell what they're thinking. What I'm thinking is it wasn't a great idea to meet them at my place. That isn't the important thing though. No, the deal breaker is Buster. He doesn't like them. He's way too polite to bark or scowl, but he doesn't like them. I think they know it cause there's no mistaking it. Anyway, I never hear from them again.

It was the junior prom all over again.

After a while, I had Buster figured out. You wouldn't guess it, but I like watching science shows on TV. A couple of years ago there was this program "partnership of man and dog." Why do dogs and people get along together so well? Good question, right? These scientists had it figured out. Dogs started out as wolves who would hang out around human places. They would eat scraps and garbage and that kind of thing. Not dining at the Ritz, but better than having to take down a dinosaur. While they're hanging around eating scraps, the boy wolves who are good with people meet up with girl wolves who are good with people, and they raise puppies who are real good with people.

Now I get to the important part. Good with people means you can read them. Dogs can tell when people are sad, when people want to play, when people want to be left alone. Then the dog does just the right thing. The dog cuddles up with his sad human, goes and fetches a stick when his human wants to fool around. And if his human wants to be left alone, the dog leaves him alone. (Dogs still aren't perfect at this.) This is what dogs do for a living; they figure out how people are feeling. It's their job. And Buster was a pro. If dogs had a company, Buster would be president.

I won't kid you. I was disappointed about the stud thing not working out and I wouldn't be getting the money I was sort of counting on. But I knew Buster was special. Special was really something, but how do you turn special into money?

I thought on it for a couple of days, and then it hits me when I'm not thinking about it: poker. Poker's a game of figuring out what the other guy is thinking, right? Is he bluffing? If I've got real good cards will a big bet scare off the other guy? Well, Buster would know what the other guy is thinking! Not only that, but I was a pretty good poker player. We played a lot in high school, and I made more money from that than delivering groceries. (I did that for a while but got fired. It wasn't fair, but that's another story.)

I got the idea on Tuesday night, not too late, maybe 8 o'clock. When I thought of it I was so excited I never got to sleep that night. Buster knew something was up. I was real excited cause this was such a great idea, and people thought I didn't have great ideas. Like when I had the business idea of finding parking spaces for people. But I needed people to work with me, and I couldn't even get Stanley to join up. (That was way before the wheelchair of course.) This was going to be different. Details are important and I wasn't going to screw it up by rushing and getting the details wrong.

I was going to be real careful, and take it step by step. The first step was I had to check out the idea. I needed to bring Buster to a poker game.

Lucky for me there was a friend I had, Arty, more a friend of Stanley's tell the truth. Arty had a poker game at his house every Friday night. I knew this cause he asked me to play once, but I had enough poker in high school and I might as well tell the whole truth, I'm nervous about meeting new people. But nervous wasn't going to stop me with this thing. So I call this guy, Arty. He remembers I'm Stanley's friend, and right off he guesses I'm calling about poker, so that was easy. The hard part was I had to get Buster in also. First I thought I'd make up some big story like I was partially blind and Buster was a partially seeing eye dog. One reason I didn't do it is cause Arty himself really was partially blind, so it wouldn't be polite. Also, Arty would know about blindness. He would know I was faking.

Anyhow, turns out getting Buster in was no problem. I just said Buster hated to be alone at night after being alone all day. Arty says sure, bring him. Arty seemed like a real good guy.

So on Friday night I show up at Arty's with Buster. Arty introduces me to the other guys. One is a real heavy guy named Marty. He was one of those heavy guys people call jolly, cause when he starts laughing his whole body shakes, and he has a lot of body. He thought it was funny we had Arty and Marty and says they should call me Smarty. I think maybe he heard me called "slow" by someone, and I sure am not as you can tell from the way I figured out how dogs understand people. So calling me Smarty maybe was his way of insulting me and he would think I wouldn't know cause I'm slow. But I let it fall off my back. It wasn't a big deal.

It turns out smart-aleck Marty is a cop, and the reason he's extra-large is he eats five or six meals a day at restaurants on his beat. He doesn't pay at the restaurants, but he tells us this was not cheating. The restaurants want him to eat there cause while he's there they feel protected. Marty says the restaurants are glad to feed him for free.

Arty himself was a bus driver, which is kind of strange cause of his partial blindness. I wondered if maybe his seeing wasn't so bad but when we played he kept the cards so close to his face they touched his nose. I didn't want to ask Arty how he could drive a bus. It wouldn't be polite; he might feel funny about it. I felt funny about it in a different way. I had to take the bus when my car was not working, which was most of the time. But I hoped Buster would make us enough money I could get a new car.

The third new guy I met was Len. He was a senior citizen. He was very senior, but he had a job as a bag boy working at FredMart, the supermarket on Central. He said he did it cause he wanted to get out and meet people. Arty told me later the company Len worked at for forty-three years didn't fill out the right paperwork, so Len retires after forty-three years and finds he is getting pretty much nothing from Social Security. Sometimes life is not funny.

We get down to playing poker pretty soon, but I'm not paying good attention. Thinking too much about Buster. No real chance for him to do any of his mind-reading in the first few hands, but I can wait. I even lose a little money. Then there's this interesting round. We're playing six card Dakota, and I have a one-eyed jack in my hand. That was wild, cause I had a heart showing. With his wild cards, Len had a possible straight flush or maybe three pair, or maybe nothing. That's six card Dakota for you; you never know where a hand could go. But I had Buster, so I knew. Len raised by a dollar, which surprised the rest of us cause our limit is a quarter for raising. That could mean he was real bad with numbers and maybe he was a bag boy at FredMart cause he was busted from being a cashier, or maybe he was trying to scare us off with a bluff. Or maybe he was trying to act as if he was trying to scare us off with a bluff, so we'd think he wasn't trying to scare us off and we'd be scared off.

Buster was sitting very quiet. He could of wandered around acting casual and glanced at everyone's hand (except Arty's cause his cards were so close to his face). No one would know. But that would be cheating, right? And anyway that wasn't the idea at all. The idea was Buster was going to tell me what was going on in Len's head. That's not cheating, right?

It was amazing the way Buster studied Len's face without

making it obvious to everyone. I mean you had to know what was going on to notice it, but there was no mistaking it. At least not to me. Buster was studying Len's face, and he had to let me know what he figured out. I was asking myself how he was going to do this. He couldn't just point his nose at Len and bark. Anyway so what he does is just look sideways at Len and give what you would maybe call a look of disapproval, like shame on you Len for lying. It was great the way Buster hid it, but there was no mistaking it.

And that's pretty much the way it went from then on. I would stay out of things when I didn't have pretty good cards, but I got it right whenever anyone was bluffing or had real good cards and was trying to bluff a bluff. Bottom line is I cleared more than $30 and everyone said this was the record. No one had ever left with more than $27. Arty thought this was kind of cool, but I got a feeling Marty didn't like it. Maybe he had the $27 record. I guess I have some mean streak cause it made me feel good to make Marty feel bad.

Len lives in the same direction as me, so we walk together for a while when we leave Arty's. I have Buster on his leash, cause that's the law, and I want Buster to respect the law. So we're walking and I'm chatting with Len but in the back of my head I start feeling bad about the game. I start asking myself did I cheat cause Buster helped me? I can't make up my mind, so I try to get Len to take half my winnings. I figure I lifted at least fifteen bucks from him, and I know Len needs it. Finally he agrees to take it, and that makes me feel good, so I don't worry any more about if I cheated.

So, anyway now I know my idea works. Poker is how Buster is going to make us rich. But now I need a big game. We're not going to get rich just taking $30 from Arty's game every Friday night. I even have a lead on how to get into a bigger game. It was something Marty said. Marty talked about a lot of stuff. He was a talker.

Most of the time with his mouth full. You would think cops would have interesting stories, shootouts with killer zombies kind of stuff, but not Marty. Restaurants seemed to be his specialty. But anyway, he mentioned there was a different poker game on Fridays. It's a poker game at the mayor's house, and the men who come there every Friday bring buckets of money.

I know you're prob'ly wondering how Marty knows about this. Turns out Marty's married to the mayor's sister, so the mayor is his brother-in-law. I wondered why Marty plays with us instead of with the mayor, then I remembered Marty is a poor starving cop. (I'm joking about the starving part.) He can't take a chance on losing big in a high stakes game.

I was kind of surprised when Marty calls me. He was fake polite at Arty's poker game, unless you consider calling me Smarty is not polite. But he didn't seem to like me that much. And then he goes out of his way to do me a favor like this. He calls and asks if I'm interested in a bigger game. I pretend I'm not a little scared and I tell him sure I'm interested. Then another surprise, he tells me he already got me invited to the mayor's house for the next game. My guess: he thinks I'm going to lose my shirt at the big game and he'll laugh about it when he hears from the mayor (his brother-in-law). But I was going to win, so I'll be the one laughing.

Just when it was sounding too good to be true, Marty adds a little detail that makes it a whole lot less too good: I would have to put $500 on the table at the start. Just to show I was serious. Marty and I both pretend this is not a big deal, but we don't fool each other.

I was so worried about how I would get the money I almost forgot the whole reason for everything: Buster. I had to figure out how to get Buster into the game. So I say to Marty $500? No problem. But I won't play unless Buster can come along. Marty gets real upset about this and says the kind of things people say when they get real upset. But he says he'll see what he can do. It seems maybe he was a pretty nice guy after all, going out of his way like that. Then I remember what he's prob'ly up to. Anyway, it didn't take long. The next day he calls me and says it's all set up. The mayor loves dogs, and he thought it was cute I couldn't stand to be away from Buster.

So there you go. Except for the detail of coming up with $500. The first thing I try I call my sister and explain by lending me the $500 she'd get all of her money back quicker. I knew she was going to say no, and I was right. That left only Stanley. I know Stanley had a lot of wheelchair money stashed away, so I call him. "Hi. How's Buster?" It's the first thing he says after I say to him it's me calling. I tell him Buster's just fine. Thanks. And I tell him I need a little favor. It's $500, but just for a few days. And I say please, please in so many words. But I guess when you have to sit in a wheelchair to earn your living you get kind of tight with cash. So he's quiet for a very long time.

I wonder if maybe he hung up, so I say, "Stanley?" He says, "Yeah, wow. That's a pretty big favor." I say again it's only for a while. I'll return it in a few days, but I really, really need it. He asks me why I don't sell something. I remind him I don't have anything worth $500. But he says, "Oh yes, you do. Sell Buster. Sell him to me. I need a dog more than you." I'm so shocked I don't speak for a little while, and anyway Stanley's still talking. He knows I won't just shut up and sell him Buster, so he offers me a deal. He says he'll give me the $500. I return it within a week everything's just like before, and I keep Buster. But I don't give the $500 back in a week, he gets Buster.

I know I'm going to have lots of money by Friday night, so I agree to the deal, and I pick up the cash from Stanley on

Wednesday, after work. So tomorrow I take a taxi to the mayor's house and meet these rich guys. I can feel my luck is turning. And there's a good sign. I found the Dremel tool in the back of my closet.

WAS THE UNIVERSE ALWAYS THERE?

The mind rebels at what other minds have fashioned. Priests and professors do not accept each other's universes but seek our acceptance of theirs.

The Seeker of Truth, a young skeptic, an inquisitress, frowns that the priests have the easier task. Their answer to all questions is faith, an answer that precludes other questions. She has no interest in these press secretaries for a deity. Their answers, always to believe, is a way of rephrasing "don't ask."

The professors dare to take questions; they bravely walk out on a limb of thin ice, giving answers up to the end of a long chain, questions linked to questions. In the spirit of the Bible, the priests do not tell us when the Universe began, where it began. The Seeker turns to a professor for the start of the Universe question chain. She starts at the beginning.

Professor: The Universe started 14 billion years ago, give or take a couple of years. You can't expect us to nail it down too precisely. Why would you want that? You want to celebrate the Universe's birthday? Sorry; maybe later. We need to make better measurements, better observations, the speed of distant galaxies, that sort of thing.

Seeker: But you're sure, you're certain that it—that the Universe—started *around* fourteen billion years ago.

Professor: I'll swear to it on a stack of Bibles. That's a joke.

The Seeker is not laughing. This is serious. She will risk professorial ire with a repetition that suggests disbelief. The Seeker puts strong emphasis on a crucial word.

Seeker: The Universe *started* 14 billion years ago?

Professor: Around then. Give or take.

The Seeker stares. The professor is trying, with no success, to hide a smirk. Why is this fun for the professor?

Seeker: What came before that? Before the fourteen billion years ago. Give or take?

The smirk is now unmistakable.

Professor: There was no before.

The professor's smirk anticipated the question and relished giving this answer. But he is not cruel; he would continue; he had only paused.

Professor: What do we mean by beginning? Think about going back in time. Let's speed through the last 5, 10 billion years, the formation of the earth, emergence of life, blah, blah. Career stuff for some, geologists, biologists, their ilk, even astronomers, but ho hum for those looking at the bigger picture, us cosmologists. The Universe grabs our attention only when we go almost all the way back fourteen billion years back. At fifty thousand years, a brief instant, after the beginning, we see things getting interesting. The Universe is filled with radiation. What you call matter doesn't really matter. (That's a little cosmologist joke.) And it's too hot for atoms. (They're recent innovations.) The further back we go the weirder it gets. Weirder meets hotter and filled with stuff that we can't produce in our best accelerators. And it gets denser. Weirder and weirder, hotter and hotter, denser and denser, until everything is infinite. Infinite! It means there's a wall in time. We can't go back any further. That's it. That's the beginning. The beginning of time. The start of the Universe!

The professor's voice had been growing louder as the Universe got weirder, hotter and denser. But now that he has reached the beginning he stops. He has a trace of perspiration on his forehead and a post-coital look of relaxation.

The Seeker feels awkward as if she has witnessed a sensitive private moment. She holds back, ceding a brief pause to the almost sacred story just related. She is having trouble with the beginning but must phrase her next question with exquisite care.

Seeker: So the Universe wasn't always there?

The professor catches his breath. He is pleased by her question, would have been disappointed if her attitude had been just slack-jawed acceptance. He smiles and responds to her question with his own.

Professor: What do you mean by "always"? Do you mean

was the Universe there *before* fourteen billion years ago?

Her face reddens. For a moment she wonders whether it was the professor's petard on which she was being hoisted, but that was unfair. He hadn't set a trap. It was her own damn fault.

Seeker: Of course! How foolish of me.
Professor: No, no. Don't be embarrassed. It's hard to get used to the idea of a beginning of time. We cosmologists have lots of fun making jokes about it.

She kept to herself sarcastic images of a rollicking cosmologist party. She would cut her temporal losses and move on to spatial confusion.

Seeker: I get it now. I really do… (although she didn't). It just takes some getting used to.

The professor does not understand her inability to understand but is not surprised. She is not his first Seeker.

Seeker: I'd like to switch to size.
Professor: Yes, size matters.

The professor blushes a deep red. He remembers too late the suggestive interpretation of this remark. He averts his eyes and is relieved when she continues with no sign she has taken offense or even noticed.

Seeker: So how big is the Universe? Do you cosmologists know?

Professor: Yes, oh yes. The Universe is almost certainly infinite.

At this point he usually adds his original witticism "Would you prefer for me to give you that in miles or kilometers?" But he is nervous about overlooking some ribald significance.

Seeker: "*Almost* certainly." So you're not sure?
Professor: We're pretty sure, but more measurements must be made.

The Seeker pictures the septuagenarian flying through trackless space with a huge tape measure.

We must measure the velocity, that means speed, with which the most distant galaxies are racing away from us. We are pretty sure, let me make that "damn sure," that we will confirm the infinite size, but it is our inviolable duty never to take anything on faith. To check, to confirm, never to assume.

When he spoke the word "faith" his expression suggested the taste of spoiled milk. Science, this alternative to faith, was what the Seeker had sought, but the certainty in her choice was thinning.

Seeker: Professor, do you cosmologists know where this infinite Universe started?
Professor: Yes, of course. It started everywhere.

The Seeker now felt new appreciation for the fable of the Garden of Eden, and thought she might want to chat with a priest.

AGENCY

Gideon Davis fooled with the apartment key at the end of the gold chain that spanned his moderate paunch on its way to the watch pocket of a tastefully muted plaid vest. The chain was anchored there by a large gold watch, a watch that was imprecise with the time but bore the name and Princeton graduation date of his grandfather.

He was distracted by the bearded workman in the blue uniform and toolbelt a little more than arm's length to his left. The man was looking down at his clipboard and up at apartment numbers. Gideon hoped that the number sought would not be his and carry a threat of bother. He tried to hurry with the key, when he noticed that to his right were two green-clad workmen crouched over blueprints. Why all the workmen? Distracted in this way he was surprised by something poking in the middle of his back. The workman was no longer on his left.

A voice emanating behind him sounded like what he would expect from a bearded blue workman.

"Probably didn't know what it feels like to have a revolver pressed in your spine, eh Gideon? Congratulations, now you do. First time for everything, eh?"

He sensed movement to his right and realized that the green workmen had abandoned their interest in blueprints and had joined the party at Gideon's apartment door. One of the new arrivals grabbed the apartment key, tugging at the chain and forcing Gideon to lurch forward to protect his vest.

As the chain tugger effortlessly opened the door he commented to Gideon, but perhaps more to the others,

"You goddamn know-it-all, tell everyone else how bad they are but can't even open your own door."

Once inside, the green men closed the venetian blinds, did a quick inspection of the apartment, and flashed the gunman thumbs up. The whole situation was a new experience for Gideon. He had read about such plights, but facing it was not the same. He felt a tension in his groin and worried but dared not look down.

The gunman's first words were not meant to be comforting.

"We're probably not going to kill you unless you force us to. We're not here to rob you. Curious?"

Gideon's voice squeaked, "Yes, why are you doing this?"

As the two others inspected the apartment in greater depth, the gunman pushed Gideon toward an armchair. Shaking with nervousness, Gideon put his hands on the chair's arms, turned himself around and gracelessly settled. He raised his eyes, as if shyly, to look at the gunman and saw that the beard was fake. This was a good sign; he knew that from crime novels. The three men didn't want Gideon to be able to identify them. If they planned to kill him this wouldn't be a worry.

His confidence in this was not total and there was already a feeling of dampness in his groin. Despite fear for his life he was concerned about staining the expensive armchair. The irony was not completely lost on him. An epidemic of moues would infest his Manhattan literary self-important confrères at the news of Gideon's death in a soiled armchair.

"Why are we doing this? The three of us are hardworking 'regular' guys. I won't tell you anything about us that I don't have to.

It will help your chance of survival."

Gideon fought back the urge to blurt out a promise that he would do whatever they wanted and would never identify them. Never. He would swear on the grave of his mother (who in fact was living with her third husband in Westchester County). The gunman continued.

"Here's the thing about us that you need to know: The three of us all want to be writers. Hell, we are writers. Underappreciated writers. We've paid vanity presses to have their minimum-wage community college illiterates process our stuff. We're sick of seeing the crap that gets published and is so goddamn inferior to our stuff. So Gid, what do writers like us do? Huh?"

After waiting for too long, Gideon realized that the man was intentionally making him uncomfortable by waiting for an answer. Frightened of saying the wrong thing Gideon went with, "I don't know." It was the wrong thing.

"You damn well do know! We send queries to goddamn literary agents who can't put down their goddamn crystal snifter of cognac to even acknowledge receiving the query."

Gideon snuck a glance at his sideboard, worried that his Hennessey XO was too easily noticed. He said nothing about the gunman's split infinitive and did his best to listen with a sympathetic expression as the gunman eased into a more narrative voice.

"The three of us bumped into each other at a reading in a bookstore. We compared out stories; it stoked our fury. We decided to meet again. The third time we met we decided to do something about the injustice of literary agents. We decided to do what we are doing now. So Gideon, think of this as the chickens coming home to roost. Cluck, cluck."

Gideon began to sense the nature of the play, but where was it going? Were they livid that he had not responded to their requests to be their agent?

"You should appreciate the care we chickens have taken. Surprise: None of us has sent queries to you. That would make it too easy for you to identify us. We have sent query requests to other agents, all different agents, all the same result: A claim that there would be a response in seven to nine weeks. Then nothing. Hey Gideon, nothing. They're telling us we don't even deserve an email rejection."

Gideon could see the fury in the face behind the fake beard, and the sound of rapid breathing. Saving his mortal coil from being shuffled off by a nervous trigger finger justified a guess at intervention.

"That might be true of other literary agents, but I always respond within a week or so."

A smile brightened behind the beard. For a few seconds Gideon thought the tide had turned, but it was only a few seconds and was washed away by the tidal wave of the excited gunman/erstwhile workman.

"Gotcha! Just what we were hoping for, you lying bag of crap! My associate in green is now looking through your computer. He says that he didn't even need a password, though—hey—you would have given it to us. Trust me.

"We'll call him Greenie-One, not his real name you understand. You're only going to get this about him: He's an expert with hacking. You know what hacking is, Gid?"

It was rhetorical. Gideon was framing an answer when the gunman continued.

"Greenie-One is going to find your file of application queries and search for your responses. Unlike you he is good at his job, and we will know soon—maybe half an hour—about your responses to hopeful writers. Gideon—this is your chance to admit that you lied. You needn't admit that you're a bag of crap. We already know that."

"Well, ummm, I get many, many queries and I'm not good with organization, so…"

"Gideon, Gideon. You really are a stupid shit. We're going to know in a few minutes how many queries you've received and how many responses you've sent. Want to amend your statement?"

Gideon looked down, saw the damp spot below the zipper of his fly and mumbled, "I lied."

"Louder, Gideon. And more explicit."

"I lied, and I'm guilty as charged."

"Good. Now we're getting somewhere. And—no need to keep you in suspense—I'm going to tell you where we're getting. But first, a question, Gid. Suppose you actually read the requested ten pages of the maiden effort of a trusting, hopeful would-be author. What would you look for that would make you want to represent the author? Huh?"

At last a shift in control, though slight, to Gideon. Two thoughts fought for attention in his head. One was that his interrogator wouldn't expect an immediate answer; he would expect Gideon to take a minute. Ahh, time to think. But think what? The second thought was that without knowing what lay ahead he didn't know what would be best for him to say. Perhaps best to claim that his standards were very high, despite the contradictory evidence that Greenie-One would find.

"Well, the judgment of writing is very subjective, and…"

"Cut the bullshit Gideon. You're making us mad."

His illusion of a sliver of control faded, replaced by a sliver of reliance in the curtain of Ivy League patter he could hang.

"Okay. I would be impressed by an author who could entrance a reader with the artfulness and finesse of the serpentine prose of

Henry James. But, by contrast, I would also greatly favor an author who hooks the reader with the verisimilitude of clearly detailed descriptions, like those of Cormac McCarthy."

"Gideon, I infer that 'succinct' is not among the qualities you admire. Jesus, I hope you can write better than you can speak. Hey, we'll know soon enough."

"So Gid, here's the plot. You're going to get a dose of your own medicine, big dose. You're going to submit a query to a bevy of literary agents, at least eight. Hope you appreciate the beauty of this Gid. You and those of your ilk in your confederation of dullards ask for the first ten pages of the proffered novel, ten pages that will never be read.

"So Gid, you're going to submit ten pages of your new novel, the novel you're going to write in this apartment, starting today, and ending within a week. Excited, Gideon?

"If you cannot write well enough to get an agent, Gid, we regretfully have to ask, should you *be* a literary agent? Should you be judging the work of others?"

"Let me share some of the logistical details with you, Gid, and please forgive me for bragging. The three of us pondered details over countless cups of coffee, fueled by our feeling about your genus. Hate is probably too strong a word for that feeling. Maybe not.

"First, you're going to plead your case only to agents you have not dealt with. Greenie-One will search your computer to handle that. Second, you're going to need to do some research—geography, synonyms, that sort of thing—but we can't have you sending out calls for help. How the hell can we handle that, you ask? Well, Gid, as long as you asked: One of us will always be looking over your shoulder. I and Greenie-Two have day jobs but will call in sick three days this week. Greenie-One has a very flexible hacking schedule, so will be here almost all the time.

"Two months after you submit, if a literary agent takes you on, we will congratulate you. We really will, but we don't think that will be Act Three. We suspect that you will join us in the rank of the rejected. At that point we will send an anonymously authored story to literary magazines, blogs, you name it Gid. In that story we will leave out the part about three thugs forcing your hand to the keyboard. We will simply point out the hypocrisy of the literary agent scam by documenting your own rejection.

"Gideon! I'm disappointed at not seeing a look of admiration. Ah well. Geniuses are rarely recognized in their own times. Let's not waste minutes lamenting the failures of society. Dinner and then writing."

The gunman first walked to the door to the apartment and fastened the safety chain. The man Gideon took to be Greenie-Two opened the toolbox and removed sandwiches and a bottle of claret.

Gideon didn't chance the social snub of refusing the implied dinner invitation but it led to the logistics of the hostage covenants.

"I don't want to be a bother, but I very much need to use the bathroom."

The dinner companion Gideon took to be Greenie-Two spoke for the first time. "Give me your phone."

He then marched de-phoned Gideon to and into the bathroom, closed the door and stood waiting just outside. Gideon was shy about such things and Greenie-Two listening at the door intimidated his digestive system. The result was an unproductive seven minutes with suggestive throat clearing from Greenie-Two growing louder.

By midmorning of the following day awkwardness had dissipated enough for Gideon, his shoulder feeling the stare of Greenie-One passing over it, had progressed enough to type *Virtue and Violence* in a new Word document.

The stare was then joined by a sharp comment, making Gideon jump.

"That's a stupid title."

The gunman approached the desk with an equally sharp counter comment to Greenie-One.

"No criticisms! No suggestions! He could claim his writing was rejected because he made changes we told him to."

Gideon felt a brief moment of false hope that his captors would fight among themselves opening an opportunity for his escape. He had read this plot a few times. Sadly for Gideon, the reality of his hostageness followed a different plot; there was no further quibbling. He was on his own, deleted *Virtue and Violence*, and stared at a blank page.

The three hostage takers had not specified what they would do if he did not cooperate, or—trying to cooperate—could produce no better than he did in the bathroom. The very desperation, the admitting the worst to himself, somehow gave him spirit to chip away at writer's block.

On the fourth day Gideon created the title, the brief description, and the first ten pages of *The Choice*, the faux first chapter of a novel of which there would be no more. He distributed printed copies to his captors, all of whom happened to be in the apartment at the time.

The three of them read, each at his own speed, each making the not-quite-conscious noises of those who read by themselves. Committed to silence they then communicated with each other through furtive looks that were hidden to Gideon.

"The Choice"

The blue-green eyes in his leathery face had
learned to distinguish the motion of the dun
tumbleweeds from the distant approach of
horses carrying strangers, potential
threats, as were all stranger. His trained
eyes squinted at the movement, the potential
threat, on the western horizon. The golden
sun, in its daily descent, was waning but
still in command, making any assumption a
dangerous guess. He had not lived to age 32
in the rough country by making guesses.

The dusty plain was flat, conceding defeat
to the green swath of the mountains to the
north only at a great distance. On the vast
colorless expanse of the High Plains the
skeletal amaranth and pigweed, waiting to
age to tumbleweeds, offered no cover. The
nearly featureless land was like a face un-
shaven for a week, with neither the bur-
nished beauty of smoothness nor the muscular
ruggedness of a beard. The cowboy was used
to making the best of the bad, of improvising, of surviving. He dismounted to wait. He
could be a statue.

His Sharps 44 carbine stood tumescent in
the dark chestnut leather scabbard hanging
vertically from straps behind the cantle and
secured to the right flank cinch behind the
right saddle fender. It represented the hag-
gling, years ago, with a saddle maker who
drew up short when the cowboy, not about to

back down in issues of his survival, commissioned a smooth rifle scabbard from sanded split-grain horsehide, not as durable as the thick leather of his saddle but serving a very different purpose. He wanted, claimed he needed, to be able to reach back with his right arm and pull the carbine out of its easily yielding lodging, with no hesitation that could cost him a few desperate seconds and therefore his life, a life that he felt not yet finished with.

Holding the rifle now, squinting to the west, he waited to the east of the horse, a sixteen hands mare. He stood with his wiry legs aligned, just behind, the horse's front legs and thereby, the cowboy hoped, invisible to whatever malevolence was approaching from the west. His wide shoulders were protected by the wide bulk of the horse's neck, while the cowboy's eyes found themselves a few inches above the horse's withers, an arrangement to ensure that whoever, whatever was approaching would see very little of him, but since solitary stationary horses were not to be found on the High Plains, would know that he was there. He did not shed the hat, the hat that made him more visible, that had a bullet hole patched two years earlier, teaching him a lesson the cowboy not one to forget would carry with him. He kept it on; the hat was crucial to shade his eyes. One of the details and decisions that his life pivoted on.

His mare was a buckskin. He was reluctant to put the sorrel, his previous mount, out to pasture but there came the time that reality and the pasture could not be put off. His reluctance at that time spoke both to how well the sorrel had served, but also to his own future, of the pasture time that would come but that he would do his damnedest to postpone. And he knew, he firmly believed, that he would do this not by the force of his fists or trueness of his aim, but with his attention to details. His horse was an important detail. How easily he was spotted was a detail; it was important he not stand out in the bleached, achromatic, washed-out flats the riding of which had become his life. The choice of a buckskin was obvious. The full socks on the legs were not a problem. The front legs were dark below the knee and the back legs along the canon bone, above the fetlock, but these would be obscured by the scrub vegetation in the land he rode. The mane was not obscured, but little could be done about that. The cowboy had spoken to stable wise men about shaving the mane. The good ones, those who knew that they did not know, gave no opinions. The cowboy did not rush to do what he didn't understand and respected the mane after thinking about its value should something go wrong with the reins.

He waited. The sun progressed west and the distant rider east.

The buckskin sensed the approach, shared the cowboy's nervousness, though not his patience, and whinnied. The distant rider had already seen them and slowed his approach to mollify the tension that felt like a vibration in the dry air between the rider and the cowboy. When the rider was within handgun distance, he tied his reins around the saddle horn and raised his hands, covered in gauntleted deerskin gloves but empty of any weapon.

The rider's sun-darkened face was mottled with the nascency of gray in the sooty grain of stubble only near the chin, and not capable of, or even attempting to hide the scar starting closer to the orbit of the right eye than to the cauliflowered right ear and disappearing under the cliff edge of the jawline. The rider wore a dark hat and clothes that carried trail dirt enough to gray the black of the cloth under them. His horse was a Morgan, larger than most of the breed, and black to complete the raft of dark the rider presented. His voice too was dark.

"I can do this hands up, but hell, you got your rifle pointed at my heart, so I figure you can trust me to lower my hands for gettin' off my horse."

The cowboy said nothing. On the High Plains silence was understood as affirmation, agreement, at least understood enough for the mounted rider to lower his hands then slowly lower his body on the side of his horse that the cowboy could see. The dismounted stranger stood still showing no sign of nervousness. Looking at a Sharps 44 would kindle a nervous fire in the business types who were setting up shop in Cheyenne and Dodge as the military personnel began to change interests. Neither of the men facing each other ignited easily, but when a spark did set them off, the fire was intense.

The stranger spoke again in a voice that was hoarse with lack of use.

"Surprised ya don't reknize me. It was in Deadwood. Time of them finding gold in the black hills. Could be wus back in '70. We wus with different outfits. Dint fight each other. Dint help neither."

The cowboy spoke for the first time.

"Three years ago. The saddle hasn't been easy on you, but yeah, I think I remember you, or you've talked me into it. But no offense I'm just going to leave this here carbine resting across my horse while you tell me, this just a lucky meeting, or you been tracking me?"

"Lucky, yeah, lucky for you. Chance to make a bundle."

"I'm listenin'."

"I work for the head of Jefferson County Cattle Company. Guy named Williams. Last name."

"Yeah, I heard rumors. He's got his hands on lots of land. Pretty much taking over the corner of the territory."

"Rough dude, Williams. Plots wus owned mosly by a bunch of small ranchers. They'd never of amounted to much. Williams offered 'em good money to find something they'd be better at. Lots of them were stubborn but got caught in a thirty caliber plague."

"Too bad. Don't like to hear that sort of thing. But nothin' to do with me."

"Could have. Maybe something with you, and a bundle of cash. Williams needs someone to head his little army."

"Why not you?"

The stranger made a grimace that he thought was a smile, showing teeth no less dark than his outfit and fang-like cuspids well suited to the face.

"Yeah, why not? Asked him that very question, I did! Said cuz he needed someone smart. Real charmer, Williams. Gonna get himself shot. Woulda been by me weren't fer two Colts 45s lookin' in my direction at the time."

"Anyway, Williams's gonna be fightin' off someone just like him, even worse. Guy from the east named Sullivan, came over from Ireland couple of years ago. Built up a gang. Saw the same thing Williams did: owning all of the Montana territory. Got no land now, but got a lot of guns and lot of fingers that like to pull triggers. Ain't no secret gonna be a war. You wanna be a general and get rich?"

"You asking if I want to work for a robber cattle baron who's killed his way to his land grab?"

"Yup. Bull's eye. Just what I'm asking. You got scruples? Keep 'em under your hat. Williams's a whole lot better'n Sullivan."

The lowest point of the sun was kissing the horizon like a shy lover draping itself in stratified curtains of amber, purple and orange as the sky darkened and provided only a backdrop for the stranger who was no more than a silhouette. The cowboy was still shielded by his horse, and still had his Sharps ready to respond to any move by the stranger that threatened, maybe any move at all. A phrase the stranger used stuck in his head, "He needed someone smart." Over the next few days the cowboy would keep that and its meaning in his head. Smart or dogged with details? Was there a difference? He spoke to the stranger without speaking an answer.

"I gotta think about it. If the thinking gets me interested, what do I do?"

"You gotta ride to Jefferson County. Not that hard. Go pretty much due north. The mountains go north-south so you'll be ridin' between 'em, and it's easy riding. Three-day ride. Be easy to find Williams; won't be easy to avoid bullets. Watch your back. Watch your front. Watch your sides."

The stranger raised his hands. It was his way of reminding the cowboy of how he dismounted. He thought he was being witty. As he lowered his hands he noted that the cowboy did not lower the carbine; it stayed leveled at him until he had disappeared into the sunset.

That didn't mean he couldn't return, steal what he could before telling Williams in Montana that the offer had been refused, so the cowboy wasn't about to bed down in the open. "He needed someone smart" echoed in his head.

It took half an hour riding in the dark to reach the best shelter he was going to find, on the leeward side of a small rise. It was a crop of dwarf birches with a few taller river dwarf birches scattered among them. The tallest around five feet, enough, but the birch root systems were shallow, a problem for racking-up the buckskin.

He chose a tall one that seemed better rooted than most and tied it with a short rope to a nearby dwarf, then tied the end of the long lead rope to the short rope, securing the other end of the lead to a bit ring of the buckskin's bridle. The horse would have to uproot both trees if it wanted to wander, and there wasn't much around to spur a horse to wander. The cowboy uncinched the saddle at the front, undid the billet strap and removed the saddle, his pillow. There wasn't much foraging, so he put a few handfuls of oats into the feedbag. He laid out his bedroll with the carbine along his left side and his Colt single action to the right of his hip where it would fall naturally to his hand if he had to make a grab for it in the dark.

He had done all the details, all that could be done. He felt safe enough to close his eyes but not his mind. "He needed someone smart." He could plead guilty to that, but Williams wanted something else, someone not burdened by too much conscience, someone willing to kill, someone willing to make excuses to himself that it was all justified. He wondered if he had become that person or maybe always was.

Susan thought that he hadn't been, that he had been, or at least once had been, good, whatever good meant to her, or meant at all. She had come from the east, a year out of college, a year into marriage, a few months a mother. Philadelphia was the past. Their lives lay in the future and the couple saw the future in the West, so she and her young husband packed what they had, gathered and borrowed, and lured by stories traveled to the Wyoming territory and set up a general store in Cheyenne.

Susan's dream was to be a teacher, she would be raising the rough humanity of the High Plains with the same devotion dished out to her infant. Building a nation and building a family. But dreams are for sleeping. In the cruel light of the Cheyenne day, spillover of the untaught rough humanity from the saloon altered Susan's future. Two cattle-drive cow hands, toxically soaked with whiskey distilled in the saloon bathtub, foundered into the store to compete in the marksmanship needed to kill a 50 lb bag of flour. In a fatal attempt that was widely judged foolish, Susan's husband sought to save the life of the flour and intervened in the shooting competition. At the trial the death was ruled an accident and the husband's actions criminally witless.

The cowboy had come to know Susan during the few months before the shooting, and she to know him.

The cowboy was working for the Cheyenne stockyard company, which gave him the title of cattle hand, but expected, and was not disappointed by, the way in which the cowboy was effective in keeping order in the disorderly town in which the marshall was different from the patrons of the saloon and brothel only by carrying a metal star.

She sensed that the cowboy was different, although it was a sensing that had to transcend words which the cowboy meted out no more with her than in a confrontation with a blind-drunk trouble-maker. She did transcend that barrier and found some succor in touching the mind of an anomaly among the mindless.

After the shooting he would spend time, not much but more than purchases would need, listening to her and loosening his miserly verbal restriction. At first, he kept the visits to only a few minutes. More than a few would fuel gossip about a widow. That threat hung over their meetings even when the cowboy chanced longer visits, visits that would quickly change tone and then end should a customer enter. Their stop-and-go interaction was thus in shards, but became important to both of them even leading the cowboy to relax his worry about wagging tongues.

Reading the shards he came to understand that she would be leaving Cheyenne and returning to the nest of Philadelphia family. Leaving was the right thing to do and, though he knew that and believed that, it surprised him to realize the intensity of his feeling about losing what little they had.

There had been a day of rain keeping customers away. The cowboy felt comfortable in the store and they talked. Both of them. What did it mean to be a good person, to do the right thing, when facing bad choices and surrounded by bad people. As the rain fell he told Susan how he saw this. Why be good if there is no reward? She could only talk about, not provide, an answer.

"The ancient Greek philosophers thought about this question a lot. What does it mean to be good. They tell us to think about how a good book is different from a good shoe. Being good means serving well in some purpose."

"And what is the purpose of a person, Susan? Do they tell us that?"

"They don't agree about it, but maybe it's to be happy."

"I can buy that. What does 'happy' mean? Means I feel good. Good means happy, and you're happy when you feel good. Susan, how does that help me decide if I should shoot a killer? These guys who went around in white togas thousand years ago have a rule book for deciding?"

"No. They talked about these matters, but never really came out with answers."

"Susan If they never had answers, why bother with what they had to say?"

"Because they make us think about these things for ourselves."

"I was already doing that, and I wasn't getting anywhere. So forget the toga boys, why do *you* think we do the right thing?"

Susan spoke with a faint smile, but was definitive in asseverating, "Because we have no choice."

She left a few weeks later. He had thought about doing something that would keep her in Cheyenne, but it would not have been the right thing and he understood that he had no choice. No choice. He had done the right thing, if he could go back he would not have done it differently, but lying in the low scrub of the High Plains with the biting night winds starting to hurry through the darkness he thought about her, about what she would think of the stark choice he now had to make. Do some good by helping Williams? Decide it was not his own fight and continue riding the High Plains finding work when he needed it. A sharp difference, a contrast as sharp as that of colors. The High Plains with its desolate white-grayness of a bleached skull. The mountains of Jefferson County swaddled in dark green and the expansive verdancy of the wide grazing transgressed by the ungodly red splashes of still fresh blood.

He heard it again in his head, Williams needed someone smart. The cowboy needed answers.

ABOUT THE AUTHOR

R. Henry Price is a scientist who considers writing an important part of a scientific career. He was a professor of physics for thirty-three years at the University of Utah, for eleven years at the University of Texas, and is now a senior lecturer in physics at MIT. He has been an adjunct professor of mechanical engineering at Utah and is coholder of three patents for micromechanical systems. He is a fellow of both the American Physical Society and the American Association for the Advancement of Science. He has a black belt in Shotokan karate and was a ski instructor, though (by his own admission) never a very good skier. He has published more than 100 scientific articles and book chapters, including twenty-nine pedagogical articles, and has authored or coauthored four books. To learn more, visit www.rhenryprice.com.